MW01675390

Immortal Choices

The Payton Adams Series, Volume 3

Tori Rayne

Published by Tori Rayne, 2021.

This is a work of fiction. Similarities to real people, places, or events are entirely coincidental.

IMMORTAL CHOICES

First edition. October 12, 2021.

ISBN: 978-0995247192

Written by Tori Rayne.

This book is written in Canadian English.

IMMORTAL CHOICES is the third book in the Payton Adams Series. I highly recommend that the books be read in order to get the maximum enjoyment from them.

There are plans to continue the series and add side stories within the Sylvan Falls/Paranormal and Supernatural Agency Universe. STAY TUNED!

The Payton Adams Series in order are:

Supernatural Secrets

Magical Mayhem

Immortal Choices

By Tori Rayne

Want to be the first to hear about special offers, giveaways and free content? Sign up for my newsletter.[1] I will also announce upcoming books on my website[2].

If you would like to contact me, you may do so at mailto:tori@torirayne.com

You may follow me on Facebook[3] and Instagram.[4] Check out my Website[5] for info on new books as well.

---

1. https://www.torirayne.com/newsletter/
2. https://www.torirayne.com/
3. https://www.facebook.com/toriraynefantasywriter
4. https://www.instagram.com/authortorirayne/
5. https://www.torirayne.com/

CHAPTER ONE

STREAMS OF MORNING sunlight flickered through the large window of Sam's living room. He woke to his body aching from falling asleep at an awkward angle. Rubbing his neck, he sat up straight. Looking to his left, he smiled when he realized Payton was curled up, having also drifted off to sleep again.

The nightmare she had woken from left her trembling. Sam knew she got little rest because of terrible dreams. Payton had mentioned being haunted by nightmares regularly.

When she woke, calling out and screaming, he went to her. He figured they would both manage to stay awake by moving to the living room to chat. He had not intended to fall back to sleep, though he welcomed the rest.

His own troubled nights, dreaming about the loss of his colleague Rick, were finally beginning to improve as he spent more time with Payton. He was constantly amazed at her strength, despite all she had been through.

Regrettably, it looked as though things were only meant to worsen with the new information Azrael and Joshua had shared with her. As if that wasn't bad enough, Payton now had a stalker as well.

Sam rubbed his face with his hands and exhaled. Glancing at the time, he realized they were late for work. He was reluctant to wake her as he gazed at Payton's peaceful expression. Her long brown hair lay against her cheek and fell onto the pillow, framing her beautiful face. The corners of her lips were curled slightly.

At least she seems to be having pleasant dreams. Sam grinned to himself. He was happy that she was there but did not like the circumstances that prompted his invitation. Sam loved that she was independent and knew that things had to feel pretty crummy for her to agree to stay with him.

He shifted a little, trying not to wake her, but Payton began to stir. He sat back, turning away to look down at the floor in front of him. Feeling Payton push herself to a seated position, he glanced over as she stretched.

Looking over at Sam, she wiped the sleep from her eyes and yawned. "What time is it?"

"Nearly nine-fifteen."

Payton abruptly stood and scratched her head, then attempted to smooth her hair. Her eyes focused on Sam's face. "I can't believe I fell asleep again! I guess I was more tired than I thought?"

Sam stood across from her and gave a half shrug. "Judging from your peaceful demeanour, I'm guessing you had no more nightmares?"

Payton shook her head back and forth. "No. I don't even remember dreaming." She grinned at him. "How do you feel?"

Sam chuckled, massaging his shoulder. "I'm a little sore from the way I fell asleep, but other than that, I'm great." A corner of his mouth lifted. He was happy that she was there with him. He wanted to help keep her safe. Part of him wondered if she slept well because he was in the room with her, but he quickly dismissed it as wishful thinking.

Sam ran both hands through his hair, letting out a sigh. "I was thinking... maybe we should tell Frank what's been going on?" he said while remaining standing.

Payton twisted some hair between her fingers, looking at Sam, bleary-eyed. "You mean about Brian?"

Running the heel of his palm across the stubble on his cheek, he said, "I mean about everything. If it's like you said, Frank may not even know about the prophecy. If he did, he might have some advice to help you with that. He also may be able to help us find out how Brian got a note into HQ. At the very least, he needs to know you are staying with me."

Payton nodded in agreement. "I'm sure Azrael has told him something by now. We haven't shown our faces in operations or our office since yesterday morning. He'll know something is wrong. To be honest, I want to get this whole stalking thing over with. I want to get back to work properly."

Sam couldn't agree more. He wished things were not so complicated right now. He watched as Payton frowned and looked away as if in thought, then moved her gaze back to him.

With a slight smile, she added, "I'll call him after I have a coffee and a shower. I need to wake up before I tackle Frank and his paternal reactions."

"Sounds good. I'll make us coffee. I'm pretty sure I have some in the house," he chuckled, "go have your shower." He headed for the kitchen to search the cupboards for coffee.

AFTER PUTTING THE COFFEE pot on, Sam headed down the hall to his own room to shave, brush his teeth, and change clothes. He had pulled on a shirt and a fresh pair of boxers; when his phone rang. He answered without glancing to see who was calling. "Hello."

"How dare you!" said an angry male voice.

Sam's hackles went up. He narrowed his eyes while the stranger continued blasting him.

"You think you can take her away from me?" the voice hissed.

Sam's ears perked as he listened for any sounds in the caller's background that might offer a clue as to his location. He thought he'd heard traffic but wasn't sure.

"Who is this?" demanded Sam.

The voice was relentless. "I'm going to kill you, Sam. And I'm going to make her watch!"

Sam yelled into the phone. "Who is this? Come and get me. I'm not scared of -" The call disconnected. Sam threw his phone onto his bed and ran both hands through his hair, huffing out an angry roar. Filled with outrage, the shifter bear side of him was on the verge of making an appearance. He clamped his fists together.

If I get my hands on this guy, so help me.

A soft knock on his bedroom door brought his awareness back to the room.

"Sam?" Payton's worried voice called out from the hallway.

Unclenching his fists, he hastily pulled on a pair of jeans and took a few deep breaths while striding to the door. He threw open the door, attempting to subdue the irritation the phone call had stirred in him.

His body tensed when he saw Payton standing in front of him, soaking wet, with only a towel wrapped around her. *Damn.* Sam ran a hand through his curls, then cocked his head. "Hey. What do you need?"

His breath quickened as his eyes darted to her dripping wet hair sticking to her bare shoulders. It was apparent she'd rushed out of the shower without even taking the time to dry herself off. It took a moment or two for everything to sink in. He was never sure if Payton read his mind or not. Though based on a previous discussion with her, he doubted she would. He prayed she had not heard his thoughts this time since he was trying hard to resist ogling her.

Looking bewildered, Payton squeaked, "I was finishing up in the shower but felt something going on in here. A lot of anger... are you okay?"

Sam swallowed hard. "Yeah. I'm fine." He rubbed the back of his neck, flitting his eyes to hers, then away again.

Her brow furrowed. "Samuel Clements. Are you lying to me?" Payton slid a hand to one hip. She studied him; her mouth down turned.

Unsure how to respond, it shocked him she had picked up his feelings from the other room. Then again, she was an empath, besides her multitude of other unique qualities. He was hesitant to let Payton know about the phone call. She had enough to worry about.

"It was nothing. I was just ranting," Sam faltered, biting his lip and avoiding eye contact.

Payton shook her head and took a step closer, scrutinizing him. He could smell the soap on her skin and found it hard to be standing so close to her. She pressed her index finger to his chest. "I heard what sounded like your raised voice. And angry energy...coming from this room...off of you. So please don't lie to me!"

It still baffled him that she heard him or felt his energy. Could she sense what he was feeling right now?

"You heard me?" he took a step back.

Payton scrunched her face. "Don't change the subject. You know how easily I pick up emotions. Now tell me, what's going on?"

Sam put his arms out to the side, "but you said you heard me? How?"

He assumed he was the only one with excellent hearing due to him being a bear shifter.

Sighing, she folded her arms. "It's not like *hearing*, exactly. It's more of a psychic feeling...," she explained before waggling her finger in front of Sam, "you're avoiding my question. Just tell me, did someone call?"

He could see that it was no use trying to keep it from her. He scratched his forehead. "Okay. Yes... Someone phoned. He was saying something about me taking you away from him. It was obviously Brian." He grimaced.

Payton pushed past him, storming across the room to his bed. Sam watched her pick up his phone and look at the caller ID. When she looked back at Sam, her face paled. "Damn it, Sam. What if he knows where you live?"

With a few long strides, Sam was in front of her. He reached to put his hands on her bare arms but stopped himself. Rubbing his hands down his thighs, he let out a low but audible groan. "I'm sure he doesn't even realize...,"

Payton's eyes flitted back to Sam's phone, ignoring his groan. When her eyes met him again, she looked fretful. "But what if he does?" Payton backed up toward Sam's unmade bed and sat down. She was shivering.

Sam couldn't tell if she was scared or cold from being wet. He didn't sense any fear coming off her. All Sam could smell was soap and Payton's own sweet scent, which he knew all too well from working with her every day.

His arms remained at his sides. "I should go see this Brian guy by myself," he grumbled.

Payton put a palm out. "No! You can't do that."

A long, awkward silence followed. Sam was getting more and more flustered by her being in his room. On his bed. With nothing on but a towel. Heaving an enormous sigh, he gazed past her. "Okay. Let's get to HQ and figure out a game plan. I might have an idea, but it means you staying the night in staff quarters."

There was a sharp intake of breath from Payton. "No, Sam! I spent six weeks living down there already. I won't..." She shook her head before fixing her eyes upon him again. "What is this idea of yours, anyway?"

Sam made eye contact with her again. He couldn't help but feel bad for the situation she was in. As much as he wanted her to stay with him, he believed HQ was the only place she would be truly safe.

"I want to lure the guy out. Let him know you are staying with me. We may catch him that way." Unconsciously, Sam's eyes drifted down across her chest and then to her long bare legs before moving back up to meet her eyes once again.

Payton's eyes widened, and she put her arms around herself, suddenly aware of her state of undress. She looked down at the towel around her and back at Sam. "Uh. I'm sorry," she frowned.

Sam's mouth twitched as Payton's cheeks turned bright pink.

She stood, and Sam stepped aside so she could get past him. "I'll go dry off and get dressed... If you promise not to do anything about my stalker until I'm done?" Payton stammered without looking at Sam again.

Sam bit his lip. "I promise. We'll talk more when you're..." Sam didn't finish as he watched Payton hurry out of the room, shutting the door behind her.

CHAPTER TWO

SAM WAS IN THE KITCHEN when his phone rang. This time, he noted the caller ID and saw that it was Frank. He answered after the second ring. "Good morning." He smiled.

There was a brief pause before Frank asked, "Sam. Where are you?"

Sam sighed, realizing neither of them had called Frank to let him know what was going on. Now he was late for work as well. He hoped Frank wasn't angry with them both.

Sam rubbed the nape of his neck. "I'm still at home. Payton is here with me. We need to talk to you, boss."

Frank paused a moment, sounding unruffled but resolute. "If it's not urgent, I suggest we chat later. I've got a case for you both...."

ANOTHER TEN MINUTES passed before a well-dressed Payton entered the kitchen with her damp hair tied in a ponytail. She grinned at Sam.

"Hey," Sam grinned back, handing Payton a cup of coffee. "Double, double, just the way you like it."

Her eyes sparkled as she took it. "Thanks, Sam. You spoil me." she gave a lopsided grin then blew on her coffee before taking a sip.

Sam stood at the kitchen counter, leaning his elbows down on it. "Frank called. He's sending us on a case outside Sylvan Falls."

Payton's face lit up. "Where is it exactly?"

Sam peered down at the phone in his hands and back at her. "Gardenvale. Have you heard of it?"

She shrugged. "No. Sounds good, though. It will be nice to get out of Sylvan Falls for a little while. What's the case?"

Sam stared down at his phone again, placing it down on the counter. His gaze met Payton's as he explained, "he's sending the file to our phones. Operations got the call last night about a guy that's been on their radar for a while."

Sam's phone pinged. Picking it up, he scrolled through the file contents. "It says here that the guy's name is Harold Johnson." He showed a photo to Payton.

She raised her brows. "The guy looks normal enough."

Sam continued reading the file out loud. "Harold was fine until about two years ago. His parents died in a strange accident that put him on our radar. They were electrocuted in their home. Not long after, Harold sold the family home and moved to a rural farmhouse, cutting off contact with everyone."

"He refused to see family and friends. He even stopped working. It seems he does some farming but manages financially due to well-insured parents and careful investments on his father's part." Sam looked up at Payton and caught her watching his face as he read. He grinned at her. "There's a little more info here, including his address."

Payton grabbed her own phone, and Sam watched as she pulled up the same file. "It says here that a young woman was found electrocuted near where Harold lives. The local media and police are saying she was struck by lightning. Operations suspect Harold had something to do with it?"

Sam bobbed his head. "Yeah. He appears to emit an electrical charge when he gets upset or angry," he read aloud.

"Or let me guess... aroused or excited as well?" Payton said with a wry smile.

WITH SAM DRIVING, THE pair arrived in Gardenvale just after midday. Payton had enjoyed the drive out of Sylvan Falls. The sun was shining, and the day was shaping up to be a good one.

Neither she nor Sam brought up the incident from a few hours earlier. She still couldn't believe that she had gone to him straight out of the shower without thinking.

Despite being very attracted to Sam, she thought it best not to act on her feelings or encourage the type of relationship that might not be allowed at The Agency.

The last thing she wanted was to have to change work partners if they were told they couldn't continue working together. The thought of not working with him each day was not very palatable. He understood her, and they got along great. She didn't want to risk losing that.

Besides, she still wasn't sure if he felt the same way about her or if he just saw her as his best friend?

Biting her lip, she looked out the passenger window as her mind wandered to the memory of Sam's face when he'd seen her wearing only a towel. She felt his desire for her at that moment but pretended she hadn't noticed.

Her thoughts were interrupted by the sound of Sam's voice. She turned her head to look at him. "Sorry? I missed that?"

Sam kept his eyes on the road. He sounded mildly amused, "I said. I wonder if this guy, Harold, knows he's being watched when he leaves his house?"

She hadn't thought about it. "Who knows?" after a brief pause, she added, "we should approach Harold with caution. Whatever we do, we can't let him feel threatened."

"I'll be careful. I don't fancy being fried, thanks," Sam said with a cheeky grin. "Hey, do you think Harold Johnson is like the guy in those comic books that can control electromagnetic energy?" He glanced over at Payton with a mischievous grin spread across his face, then moved his eyes back to the road.

Payton smiled from ear to ear at Sam. She knew he was just being light-hearted and was probably as embarrassed as she was about their earlier encounter.

She couldn't believe her luck in meeting Sam and getting to work at The Agency. Her life was far from perfect, but it had never been, anyway. The obstacles standing in the way of her being truly happy weighed heavily on her.

Her friendship with Sam helped make everything more tolerable. Sam had a way of making her smile, even at the silliest things. When she was with him, she forgot all about the prophecy, the dangerous power inside her, and that she was the only Immortal Witch Guardian alive.

With Sam, she could be herself.

Payton sighed as she scanned Sam's profile. He glanced sideways, taking his eyes off the road briefly.

"What?" she grinned.

"What do you mean what? You were sitting there daydreaming...so do I assume you don't think he is a magneto kind of guy?" he quipped.

Payton shook her head as she got a flash of Sam's big brown eyes before he looked back at the road. Feeling flustered, she responded, "I don't know... Maybe?"

FINDING HAROLD JOHNSON'S farm was more straightforward than they expected. The large farmhouse and surrounding area looked serene as they pulled down the driveway. "Looks like no one's home," Sam noted.

"Maybe he parks his vehicle around back," said Payton as she tuned in psychically, "I feel like someone is home."

Sam parked the SUV just in front of the house and turned off the ignition. "Good, let's hope he doesn't mind us dropping in."

Moments later, the pair were standing at the front door. Payton knocked and waited while she tuned in to get a sense of how many people might be inside. She put up one finger. Sam nodded in response.

After about a minute, a thin, casually dressed man in his late twenties opened the door. "Yes?" he said in a monotone voice.

"Harold Johnson?" asked Payton, taking in the pasty-skinned, fair-haired man.

The man's jaw tensed. "Yes."

Payton smiled. "We are with an organization called the Paranormal and Supernatural Agency. May we speak to you for a few minutes?"

She held up a business card.

He glanced at the card, then taking it, he shoved it in his back pocket before stepping back to welcome them inside. The pair waited expectantly for a couple of beats before Harold ushered them into a sitting room, rubbing his palms together. He took a seat in a chair across from the two of them.

"So, what can I do for you two?" he gulped, looking uneasy.

Payton took a moment to survey the room. It was sparse in decor. There was a lack of technology of any kind. Looking at Harold, she could feel his anxiety. She stayed alert in case she needed to use magic to keep herself and Sam safe.

"Thank you for seeing us, Mr. Johnson," Payton spoke in a soothing voice.

"Call me Harold," the man said politely.

"Okay. Harold. My name is Payton, and this is my partner Sam." She motioned with a wave of her hand toward Sam, who so far had been watching in silence. "Our organization tracks unusual occurrences or events."

Harold's Adam's apple bobbed. "What occurrences do you mean?"

Payton gestured with her hands as she spoke. "Supernatural or paranormal happenings. We have tracked something to this area and would like to ask you about it."

Harold rubbed his hands up and down his thighs. "Tracked something? Like what?" his eyes filled with panic.

Payton didn't like the feelings she was picking up from him, and judging by the mix of colours in his auric field, he was on high alert. "Well," she said, drawing the word out. "Let me ask you a question?"

Harold's eyes darted between her and Sam. He nodded, "Ok. Sure."

She raised her eyebrows. "Do you believe people can have paranormal or supernatural abilities?"

Some of the tension in Harold's shoulders eased. "Yes, I do... why?" he responded, tucking his hands under his thighs.

"We... I mean, my partner, Sam, and I help people who have supernatural abilities. We protect them and assist them with understanding what is happening to them. Do you understand what I am saying?"

Harold bounced one foot nervously on the floor, "yes, I think so."

Payton tilted her head to one side. "Do you feel you have supernatural abilities?"

Harold brought his hands out from under his thighs. He held his palms, facing one another in front of him. Blue sparks flickered briefly between his palms as he looked at his hands. "I think so, yes."

Payton was still unsure about his ability to control the electromagnetic energy inside him and spoke as calmly as possible. "Good. Now that we know you have special abilities, can I ask you some questions?"

Harold nodded, putting his hand's palm down on his thighs.

Payton studied his face carefully as she spoke. "The death of your parents, can you tell me about that?"

Harold trembled. Sam and Payton gave him reassuring smiles. Sam's voice was softer than usual, "Hey, buddy...you okay?"

Harold's eyes were moist as his bottom lip quivered. "I didn't mean to do it."

Sam leaned forward, putting his elbows on his knees. "Didn't mean to do what? Can you explain what happened?"

Looking away, Harold's face darkened. "I had been outside a couple of days earlier, putting away some tools that had been left out. It was raining... Suddenly, a bolt of lightning hit not more than a foot away from me. I felt it hit the ground, and it threw me back." Harold ran his hand through his hair, then wiped his brow. "I felt fine after, energized even. I didn't tell anyone about it." He hung his head, reliving the memory of what happened. Tears rolled down his cheeks as he closed his eyes.

A few seconds later, he continued speaking. "Then, I was helping my father with some electrical repairs."

Payton tuned in to his thoughts to see if he was telling the truth. His mind was a jumbled-up mix of memories and ideas he was voicing to himself continuously. He hated himself for what he'd done, and it had messed him up in a big way.

"What happened when you helped your father, Harold?" Payton asked. Her eyes flitted to Sam and back to Harold.

Tears continued to flood Harold's eyes. He wiped at them. "I thought he was taking too long to get the rewiring of the kitchen light done. I got impatient and a bit gruff with him. Then when I put my hands on the metal ladder that I was holding, I saw a blue light come from my hands. It shot up the ladder, hitting my father."

"The next thing I knew, he was on the floor. Then my mother came into the kitchen. She screamed when she saw him." Harold's body shook with emotion. "I went to grab hold of her. I wanted her to call for help. The blue light came out of my hands again and hit her. They both died right there. I didn't mean to do it... I didn't know I would... I'm sorry," Harold sobbed. His shoulders moved up and down as he wept. Small blue bolts of energy crackled as they moved around his body.

Payton wished she had made Sam wait in the car, not that he would have listened, mind you. She didn't want Sam to be hurt. Judging from Harold's lack of control over his newfound ability, there was a significant risk.

Silence filled the space between them as the Agents waited for Harold to compose himself. Payton could hear his panicked thoughts go to the woman who had died close to their location.

Harold looked over at Payton, his eyes pleading with her. "What will happen to me?"

Sam and Payton both shook their heads. "We will do our best to help you get this ability under control. We just don't want anyone else to get hurt. Harold, is there anything else you want to tell us? Did you accidentally hurt someone else with your ability?" asked Payton.

He frowned and rubbed his hands on his thighs in a quick back-and-forth motion. Payton tuned in to his thoughts and saw the moment he was reliving. He and a young woman had been making out. The next thing Payton saw was the blue light leaving Harold's hands when he touched the victim's face. He had killed her by accident, but he would still have to pay for his crime. Which meant they had to take him back to HQ with them.

Payton wondered if she would need to use magic to subdue him. Harold avoided eye contact and shook more violently than before. Payton sideways glanced at Sam, grimacing.

Harold's head dropped. He stood up. Sparks came off his hands, arcing out a foot or so from them.

Both Payton and Sam stood, moving away quickly.

Sam put his palms up. "Hey, we will not hurt you. We only want to help you. No one else needs to get hurt."

Payton readied herself, hoping things would not escalate further. "We will do our best to help you, but we need you to trust us, okay? We need you to come with us to our facility where we can help you." She forced a smile.

Harold scowled. "I didn't mean to hurt anyone!" He looked from Sam to Payton and shook his head, backing up. His hands continued to give off sparks of electrical energy. "Why should I go with you? I didn't do any of this on purpose. I didn't ask for any of this," he gulped.

"How long do you think it will take the police to figure out that you were the last one seen with that young woman? If the human police arrest you, more people will be hurt. We can't have that. If you come with us, we can help you," Sam said, stepping around in front of Payton.

Payton stepped to one side, annoyed that Sam was endangering himself, trying to protect her. She pushed past Sam and swung her hands out with palms facing Harold, putting a force field of energy around him in one quick move, causing his arms to be locked to his sides. He attempted to struggle, but with his hands against his hips, he could not respond to Payton's magic.

She heard an audible exhalation from Sam but kept her eyes on Harold. "If you will come with us, everything will be explained to you. We are the only people that can help you," Payton stated.

Harold stopped struggling as he appeared to weigh his options.

Payton continued to hold him in the grip of her magic. "What we are offering you is better than what is happening now. I know you don't want to live in isolation."

The man nodded and hung his head. "What does this organization want to do to me?"

"The people at The Agency want to see why you have this power. They will help you figure out a way to live with it. You are a danger to others as long as you don't have control over your ability. They will not do anything you don't want them to do. I promise," Payton explained.

WHEN THEY REACHED THE Agency HQ, Payton and Sam escorted Harold to Dr. Mary James in the medical lab.

Dr. James was a five-foot-four-inch woman with bright eyes and a dainty nose. The doctor barely acknowledged Payton and directed her questions to Sam. Payton did not know her supernatural ability and didn't find the woman particularly friendly toward her.

She'd had no dealings with Dr. James so far. Still, judging from the woman's behaviour toward her, she likely would avoid any future contact if possible.

Payton continued to hold Harold in a bubble of magical energy but allowed him some limited movement of his hands.

Sam filled the doctor in on Harold's superhuman ability and stepped back as the doctor rifled through a cabinet, bringing out a pair of gray gloves and walking over to Harold.

Dr. James met Harold's nervous gaze. "Hello, Mr. Johnson. It's nice to meet you." She held out the gloves to him. "The medical team here created these gloves. As long as you are wearing them, it will help nullify the electromagnetic charge you give off. It isn't a cure, but it will help keep everyone safe until we figure out why you have this ability." She leaned forward and placed a glove on each of his hands. They appeared to bond themselves to his hands. Dr. James spoke aloud without looking at Payton directly. "You can release the spell. He can't hurt anyone now."

Payton pursed her lips, and with a wave of her hands, she stepped back, releasing the hold on Harold.

Sam stepped next to Payton and asked, "do you need us to do anything else before we go?"

Dr. James looked Sam up and down, then licked her lips salaciously. Something Payton was used to witnessing but disliked it nonetheless. Something about the doctor unsettled her. "I have it from here. Thanks for bringing him in." She batted her lashes at Sam, then motioned to Harold. "If you would like to come with me, Mr. Johnson, we have some things to go over. Then we'll get you settled in. You will stay with us for a while." She led Harold away from them.

Payton turned to walk away, rolling her eyes. Not that the good doctor would have noticed Payton's reaction. She was too busy leering at Sam over her shoulder as she walked away with Harold.

"She's new here," Sam commented as they walked away. "I haven't seen her before."

Payton scowled. *I don't trust that woman*, she thought. Trying to hide her suspicions about Dr. James, Payton glanced at him with a wry smile. "Yes. I think she *is* new... I can also see that she has a thing for you," she teased.

Sam brushed off the comment. "Nah, you imagine things. She was speaking to both of us." He headed down the hallway, Payton walking alongside him.

"Sam, I can read minds...trust me, she thinks you're hot," Payton rasped, trying not to sound jealous.

Sam studied her.

Payton sighed as they reached Frank's office door. Sam put an arm around her shoulder and squeezed. "You know you're my girl, right?" he said with a crooked grin.

Payton avoided eye contact and knocked on Frank's door.

If only, she thought.

"HELLO. GLAD TO SEE you two. How did it go with the case?" Frank smiled at them.

"No problem. Harold is in the medical lab now. He seemed to want the help," said Sam.

Payton put up a finger. "What happens with someone like Harold if he doesn't cooperate or can't be let back out into the world?"

Frank clasped his hands on his desk and looked over at them both with interest. "He would be sent to the rehabilitation facility in the Yukon Territories. Life would be limiting for him, but it would keep people safe."

"You mean because we would lock him up in a cell?" Payton made a face.

Frank moved his head from side to side. "Fortunately, that doesn't happen often, but you are correct. We would have to contain someone who refused to be helped. Now... I understand you two wanted to talk with me about something? Why don't you fill me in?" he asked, changing the subject.

Sam gave a quick look toward Payton before responding. "As I mentioned on the phone, Payton is staying with me at the moment."

Frank raised one brow, eyeing them both. "And why is that?"

Payton smoothed the back of her head and glowered. "I'm being harassed. I've received threatening notes at my home. Sam offered to let me stay with him until we catch the guy."

Frank leaned forward in his chair. "Do you know who is leaving these notes?"

Payton nodded. "The guy we picked up the gramophone from. His name is Brian Thomas." She explained everything that had caused her to think it was Brian.

The tiny lines around Frank's eyes creased a little more than usual. His lips pursed.

"Payton received a note from him at work... on her desk. We think someone in The Agency is helping him," offered Sam.

Payton shrugged with her hands out, "that would be the only way he'd get a note onto my desk."

Frank tapped his chin with his fingers as he thought. "We have hired many new people in the last couple of months because of the increase in crime in town. I didn't vet them all personally. I'll talk to the department heads and find out if they have noticed anything suspicious among their employees... I'm sorry this is happening, Payton."

Payton pressed her lips into a frown. "There's more, I'm afraid. Were you aware of a prophecy regarding me?"

"Prophecy?" Frank asked, puzzled.

Payton told him what she had learned from Azrael and Joshua about the sword of power and the prophecy that told of her being the only one able to wield it.

Frank let out a massive sigh, leaning one elbow on his desk. He put his hand to his forehead for a moment. "I wondered why Azrael was behaving more aloof than usual. He left in a hurry the other day with no explanation." A line appeared between his brows. He looked directly at Payton. "I assure you; he didn't share any information about the prophecy with me."

He shook his head. "When I met you for the first time, I told him about you. Azrael then told me you could be Immortal. He said I should not reveal what I knew about your family. All this information you now know, anyway."

Sam cleared his throat, interrupting, "the prophecy aside, we need to do something about Brian before anything else happens. I don't like him threatening Payton. I know she's Immortal, but she can still be harmed. We need to take care of this guy. The sooner we get to him, the better."

Frank nodded in agreement. "I'll send a team around to Brian's home. I think you are too close to the situation to tackle this yourself. Just keep Payton safe... He's human, isn't he?"

"We think so but aren't sure," Payton shared.

Frank thought for a moment before adding, "maybe I'll call Chief Ken and have him go by and visit Brian first. Once we have him in custody, we can learn more about who is working with him."

Payton was glad that Frank wasn't allowing Sam to go after Brian. She feared what Sam might do to the man. Or what Brian might do to Sam.

She got up from her chair.

Frank pressed his lips together. "Be careful, Payton. If Brian has someone at The Agency helping him, you don't want to reveal where you are staying."

Sam rubbed his chin. "Actually, boss, now that you mention it. I was thinking..."

Payton sat back down while Sam and Frank discussed their plan to apprehend Brian. It took some persuading, but Frank finally agreed to Sam's plan. Payton would go home with Sam like they had already planned.

Meanwhile, Frank would arrange for a couple of Agents to watch Sam's house overnight. With all three in agreement, Sam and Payton stood to leave.

Before they could leave his office, Frank put a palm up and cleared his throat. They both gazed at him. His expression was kind, but Payton sensed genuine concern from him.

Frank's voice was soft. "I can see that you both have become quite fond of one another. Be careful that your feelings don't get you both into trouble."

Payton's cheeks burned. She was too embarrassed to look over at Sam, but she stood close enough to notice his body tensed next to hers.

CHAPTER THREE

IT WAS NEAR QUITTING time, so it surprised Payton when Sam's phone rang, with Frank giving them another case. Sam put the call on speaker so Payton could hear.

"There's been an attack on a couple of college kids in town. I think it's a first-time shifter merging situation. I want you to find him and bring him in."

"Sure thing, boss," said Sam, hanging up the phone. He knew it was essential to find the new shifter before he killed someone. He turned to Payton. "You up for going on another case today?"

"Absolutely." Payton stood ready to go. The day was turning out far busier than usual. She'd barely had time to think about the threats Brian had made to her and Sam.

ONE POLICE CRUISER and a few onlookers were on the scene at the college library when Payton and Sam arrived.

Sam approached the crowd and asked aloud, "what's happened?"

A skinny kid with glasses looked up at Sam, then over at Payton. He adjusted his glasses as his cheeks reddened. "Some guy on steroids beat up some jocks. He got away, and the police are still looking for him."

Sam nodded, looking around at the scene. A couple of ambulance crews were still tending to the victims of the attack.

Payton motioned toward the scene. "Did you see anything?" she asked the bespectacled young man.

The kid shook his head. Payton thanked him and joined Sam, who had already taken a few steps away.

As they moved closer to the scene, Payton saw a fit, black-haired female police officer standing near an ambulance. She also couldn't help but notice Sam's eyes flashed with recognition as they approached the woman. Payton felt a significant and unpleasant change in Sam's energy. He bristled when the officer also recognized him.

"Hey. Fancy meeting you here." The policewoman had a toothy grin. Looking nonchalant, she glanced over at Payton, then back to Sam.

"What have we got?" Sam asked, looking past the woman to the crowd of onlookers.

Clueless to Sam's disregard, the officer motioned with her notebook and pen toward two young men being taken care of by EMTs about five feet away. "Looks like those two idiots picked the wrong guy to harass. From what I'm told, they've been picking on a kid named...," she looked at her notepad and then back at Sam, "Chace Fornier. He lost it on them and beat the crap out of them."

Sam put his hands in his pockets and nodded in acknowledgement. "I have to find this kid before anyone else gets hurt. Do any of the witnesses know which way he went?"

The officer gestured and winked. "I can do you one better. He left his knapsack. It had his library card in it. I'll give you his address." She jotted it down on a piece of paper in her notepad and passed it to Sam.

"I was going to head there next, but it looks like this case *isn't* one of ours. These strange cases always give me nightmares. I don't know how you do this stuff," the officer divulged.

Payton noticed Sam's jaw flex. She watched him glance down at the address. "Thanks for the help," he said, then added in a bitter tone, "It's not a terrible job if you're broad-minded."

Payton continued to watch the interaction, silently shocked by Sam's response.

The policewoman put a hand to her hip, squinting at Sam. "Sure... I'm open, but some things are just... hard to accept... You know? There's a reason I work with regular humans over at the police department. It beats the stuff The Agency gets up to."

The woman reached out and placed a hand on Sam's bicep. He pulled away from her, and Payton could have sworn she heard a low, angry growl erupt from his chest.

Oblivious, the woman turned to walk away, then stopped and looked over her shoulder. "Hey, Sam?"

"Yeah?" he peered at her, looking unimpressed.

"Nice to see you again." She smiled and waved over her shoulder.

Sam gave a single nod and turned his back to her. Payton was eyeing him with a look of curiosity. "What kind of supernatural is she?"

"She has x-ray vision or something like that. We've met a few times out in the field," he grunted. The hostility from Sam toward the woman was palpable. Payton sensed there was more to it but didn't want to pry.

THE FORNIER HOME LOOKED like every other house on the street. The neighbourhood was quiet and relatively upscale.

"Let's just hope we don't have a problem taking him with us," said Sam as they approached the front door.

Payton frowned. "Is that really necessary?"

Sam raised his brows. "Trust me, it's better than the alternative. At The Agency, he has a chance of a more or less normal life. They can help him adjust to being a shifter." Sam knocked and waited. He felt sure he'd caught the scent of a shifter when the door was opened by a middle-aged woman with high cheekbones and a pointed nose.

Sam smiled at her, "Mrs. Fornier?"

"Yes?"

"My name is Sam Clements. I'm looking for Chace?"

She eyed Sam through narrowed eyes. "What do you want with Chace?"

He could hear movement in the house and hoped she wouldn't make this more complicated than it needed to be.

"Look, I think you know I'm a shifter. I sense you are as well. If you let me speak to Chace, I can help him. I'm not with the Shifter Council. I am with The Agency."

Mrs. Fornier took a step back, putting one hand to her chest in a look of silent shock. Sam and Payton stepped forward, closing the door behind them. Looking to their left, they saw a young man sitting on the sofa.

Sam stepped closer to the young man, keeping his hands at his sides. He could see that Chace was frightened. Not wanting to spook him, he remained motionless.

Glancing sideways at Payton, Sam hoped she would know what he needed without him saying it aloud.

He felt relieved when Payton gave a silent nod. "Mrs. Fornier, can we talk in another room, please?" Payton asked, ushering Chace's mother into the kitchen.

Sam observed the young man. "Chace?" Before Sam could move closer, Chace lunged from the sofa and ran toward the back door, flinging it open, then bolted for the backyard just as Sam had expected.

Crap. Sam knew what was coming next. He swiftly pulled off his shirt and pants to keep his clothing from being torn to pieces. Chace, however, shifted clothing and all, leaving his ripped and shredded clothing on the lawn.

Sam knew the only way he would get through to Chace was to shift as well, and he wasted no time doing so. Within seconds Sam bear made his appearance and stood in front of Chace, who had shifted into a brown bear and stood growling at Sam.

Chace was a good half a foot shorter than Sam but was formidable nonetheless. Sam lunged at the bear and tackled him to the ground. Chace struggled, but Sam was stronger.

Sam-bear sat on top of Chace-bear, holding him down, showing no further aggression. When Chace realized he was not under attack from Sam, he eased off in his struggle.

Several minutes passed before Chace shifted back to his human form. Sam jumped up and turned back to his human self right away, then offered his hand to help Chace off the ground.

"I'm not here to hurt you, kid. I'm here to help," said Sam.

Chace scrutinized Sam. The young man was still shaking from the adrenaline rush. "Who are you anyway?"

Sam explained, "I'm with an organization that helps people with special abilities. As a shifter myself, I think I can help you."

Chace's voice shook with emotion, "I don't know what's happening to me. I,"

Sam smiled. "Let's get dressed, and we'll have a chat."

CHACE AND SAM WENT back inside, where Sam pulled on his clothing and waited for Chace to get dressed. Sam gave Payton a look of gratitude as she and Mrs. Fornier returned to the room and took a seat. Payton smiled sweetly as she took a seat next to him.

Ten minutes later, Chace sat across from the Agents with hunched shoulders. "Who's going to tell me what's happening to me and why?"

Mrs. Fornier had tears in her eyes as she spoke first, "Chace, I should be the one to tell you." She placed her hands in her lap, twisting a tissue between them. "There is no easy way to say this... Your father and I should have told you earlier..." She shook her head, looking down at her hands, the guilt and pain clear on her face. "I am the same as you. But I've learned to control it."

Chace's eyes blazed with anger. "Wait! What? You're a shifter, and you didn't think to tell me? Not once in nearly twenty years did you think to say, hey son...you're a shapeshifter? My God, mom! What were you thinking?" he snapped.

Mrs. Fornier cringed and sniffed into her tissue.

Sam waited a moment and then put up his hand. "Chace, if I may. I don't think that getting upset with your mother is going to help the situation. I'm sure she thought she was doing the right thing."

Mrs. Fornier nodded and looked at her son, her eyes pleading for forgiveness.

Sam continued to speak, placing his hands on his knees. "What happened to you today is what we call the merging. It's normal for shifters about your age. I'm guessing that today was the first day that you shifted?"

Chace nodded, looking down at his hands, turning them over and examining them. He brushed the hair from his brow, looking over at Sam. "I had some dreams about being a bear but never expected it to happen in real life." He shook his head as his eyes became moist. His eyes darted to his mother. His lips parted as though he was about to say something. Instead, he looked down at his lap and wiped his eyes.

After a brief pause, he looked over at Sam and asked, "When did *you* first...?"

"Shift?" Sam asked.

"Yeah... Shift." Chace shrugged.

Sam leaned forward with his elbows on his knees. "When I was a little younger than you. A drunk driver killed my parents. I was staying the night at a friend's house. His family were humans, and I don't think they knew any shifters back then."

"When his parents came and told me what happened, I became pretty upset. I accidentally shifted in front of my friend's parents. When it happened, they panicked and went to call the police, so I ran away."

"I lived on the streets for about six months before a PSA Agent found me. It was the best thing that could have happened. I didn't understand the changes inside me, and I was pretty angry about losing my parents. He saved me from doing God knows what with my life. I'm glad he found me."

"The Agency has become like a family to me. Being a shifter is a lot of responsibility. It made me grow up pretty fast, and it made some things more of a challenge. Still, it is what it is." Sam gave a half shrug and smiled at Chace.

Chace frowned. "I'm sorry to hear about your parents." After a few moments, he spoke up again. "It's just... I have so many questions, you know? I mean, how did this happen?" He looked over at his mother. "You never shifted in front of me. I did not know. Is dad a shifter as well?"

Mrs. Fornier whispered, "no. Only I am. We didn't know when or if your shifter side would show itself. We hoped it wouldn't, but of course, that was just wishful thinking." She closed her eyes and shook her head slowly.

Sam glanced at Mrs. Fornier, then at Chace. "It's clear that your mother regrets not telling you she is a shifter. I hope you won't hold it against her. If I could have my parents back, I would do whatever it took to show them how much I care."

Chace nodded. "I get why my parents kept it from me, but it would've been nice to have a heads up, you know? I mean, I could have killed those idiots at school. I couldn't control it, once the bear...." He flinched at the word. "Once the bear came out... I almost snapped the guy's neck."

Sam interjected, "But you *didn't* kill him, and that tells me you are stronger than even *you* realize. Cut yourself some slack and just move forward, knowing that you don't have to go through anything alone. I know it's tempting to just keep everything in and try to cope with the changes on your own. But you aren't alone. If you need someone to talk to about what you're going through, I'm here. I can relate, believe me." Sam was glad that they found Chace without incident.

The young man was fortunate that his parents were as supportive as they were. He hoped Chace would accept being a shifter when he understood more about it.

Chace looked down at his hands again. He shook his head. "What will happen to me? How do you manage? How do you keep friends when you are like this?" he asked Sam.

Sam sat back. "I have a few friends that don't judge me for being a shifter. Most of them are unique people that work for The Agency. It helps to have a great work partner and best friend as well." He tilted his head toward Payton, who he could feel watching him.

He gestured with one hand, "I wouldn't stress about friends. Some people won't be safe to tell, and others will embrace you and your bear. Really, it's not as bad as you may think. You'll learn to control the bear and only let him out when it's safe, to protect yourself or others. I know you'll do fine. You're a good guy."

"We will do what we can to help you, but you will need to come with us to The Agency for now. The organization helps people like us. The Agency staff can teach you how to control your shifting. When you get a handle on it, you can work for us or go on with your life."

Sam watched as the young shifter sat back, looking a little more relaxed. All three of them glanced at the front door when they heard a car door slam outside. Sam stood. Chace and his mother both got up. Mrs. Fornier walked toward the front door as it opened.

"Dad. Thank God," Chace exclaimed, striding toward his father.

"Honey, he shifted," Mrs. Fornier blurted before she burst into tears. Without hesitation, Mr. Fornier embraced his wife while looking at his son. His eyes went wide. "What did you do, son? Please tell me you didn't kill anyone?"

Chace stared at his father with his mouth open.

Payton strolled over to them as Sam piped up, "Mr. Fornier. My name is Sam Clements. Your son has killed no one, but he has hurt a couple of young men at his college. I'm with the Paranormal and Supernatural Agency here in Sylvan Falls. I'd like to take your son with me and help him. When he has a handle on his abilities, he can return home."

Mr. Fornier released his wife from the hug and put his hand out to shake Sam's and Payton's hands.

"Sam here is a shifter too." Mrs. Fornier said as she stood next to her husband.

Mr. Fornier kept his arm around his wife's waist.

He looked at Sam and Payton. "I've heard of The Agency. My wife told me about it when we met. She's stayed off their radar. I was hoping our son would as well." He frowned and turned to Chace, who still looked like he was in shock. "Son, I'm sorry we didn't tell you before. Your mother and I love you." His father shook his head and moved toward Chace with his arms stretched out to hug his son.

Afterwards, Chace stepped back and turned to look at Sam and Payton. He still appeared to be in shock but seemed to realize his options were limited. He motioned to the stairs with this thumb. "I'm going to go grab a few things, and we'll get out of here. I want no more trouble."

CHAPTER FOUR

PAYTON SAT AT HER DESK waiting while Sam sat at his desk next to her, filling out the report on Chace. He looked up when Mark and Alex stepped inside the office with coffee in hand. Mark smiled at them.

"We just got here and grabbed some dinner. We thought we'd head out with you two so we can watch Sam's house tonight," Mark smiled, sounding chipper.

"I appreciate that, guys. Sorry, you both have to work overnight, though," Sam grimaced.

Alex shrugged. "We don't mind. It's the least we can do." With a sheepish expression, he glanced at Payton. "I'm sorry about hassling you to go out with me. I never meant to upset you. Frank told us what has been happening, and I just want you two to know that you can trust us."

Sam had known Alex and Mark for a long time. The pair had even worked alongside him and Rick once or twice. He had no problem with either of the Agents until Alex began harassing Payton to go out with him. It looked as though Alex knew better now that Frank had filled him in on Payton and her stalker.

Payton smiled at Alex, looking much friendlier toward him than she had been in recent days. "Consider it forgotten. I am just glad you both will be our lookout tonight. I hope this whole thing will be over soon."

Sam stole a glance at Payton's profile and felt content in knowing that she was allowing him and others to help her. Payton didn't seem to understand that to him; she was more than a work partner. He considered her his best friend and would do anything to keep her safe.

Sam finished what he was doing on the computer and stood up, ready to leave. "Let's head out. I'm going to stop for takeout for Payton and me. We'll meet you back at the house?" he said, looking at Mark.

Mark nodded. "We'll make sure there is no one skulking around the place. See you when you get home."

PAYTON AND SAM WAVED to Mark and Alex before heading inside with Thai takeout. It had been a long day, and all Payton wanted to do was eat, shower, and head to bed with a book to read.

Sam helped serve the food, and the pair sat at the kitchen table, eating in silence for the first ten minutes.

Watching Sam, she could see he was avoiding eye contact, and Payton sensed something troubled him.

"Is everything okay?" she asked.

Sam scowled as he explained. "I'm bothered by something that happened when we got back to HQ with Chace."

Payton's brow creased. She had gone directly to their office, so it couldn't have been anything she did or said. "What happened?"

Sam put down his fork and placed his hands on the table. "When I took Chace to meet Dr. James, she asked me out...but made it clear what she wanted...you get the picture?"

He didn't look happy about the offer, and Payton guessed that the encounter with Mary James had him feeling out of sorts, but there had to be more to it. She narrowed her eyes at the thought of Sam being propositioned by another woman.

"Seriously? I knew she had the hots for you... but that takes some nerve. What did you say to her?" she prodded.

Sam scratched his cheek and hesitated before responding. "Don't be upset, but I told her we are involved. I figured it was the best way to shoot her down without too much trouble?"

Payton felt a swirl of excitement at the mention of such a thing. Embarrassment quickly replaced the feeling, then concern. Could Sam tell that she was crazy about him? Was it clear on her face? She bit her lip.

"I'm not upset at all. I'm...it's fine," Payton stammered, looking away.

Sam chuckled, and Payton sensed he was also feeling a little embarrassed by the admission. She quickly added without thinking about it, "If she is a spy for Brian and he thinks we are an item, that will really piss him off."

Sam chewed the inside of his cheek, suddenly looking worried. "Damn. I didn't think about that."

Payton waved her hand dismissively. "It won't matter. It may benefit us. So long as I am here with you and not alone, we should be fine... Right?"

Sam folded his arms and sat back in his chair, resolute. "I don't have any intention of letting you go home until we catch him."

His protectiveness touched Payton. "I'm sure we'll get him soon. Then the biggest thing I have to deal with is catching Lucius," she tried to sound reassuring but was now even more worried about what Brian might do.

She watched as Sam gazed back at her with a look that made her feel a little weak in the knees. *Pull yourself together, Payton.*

She got up to put her plate in the dishwasher, then snuck a glance at Sam. He was looking down at his plate, running a hand through his hair. She quickly tuned in to find that he felt as flustered as she did.

"I'm going to have a shower and head to bed," Payton said softly, moving to stand next to Sam.

He looked at her, his eyes twinkling with affection. "Have a good sleep," he murmured.

Payton wished him a good night and left the room, hoping one day she could act on her feelings for Sam but knowing there were more pressing matters to attend to first. The last thing she wanted to do was put him in more danger.

THE ROOM WAS DARK WHEN Payton woke, disoriented by the sound of the house alarm. She reached for the lamp at her bedside and accidentally knocked it further out of reach. Sitting up, her body was on high alert as adrenaline coursed through her.

She leapt out of bed, grabbed the lamp with both hands, and turned it on. Looking around the room, she saw she was alone. Her bathroom door was closed. She tried to remember if it had been open when she went to bed. Tuning in, her psychic senses didn't pick up anything or anyone nearby.

Taking a deep breath, she wondered if Mark and Alex were still outside watching the house. Wouldn't they hear the blast of the alarm as it continued to blare?

Payton darted for her closed bedroom door and pulled it open, prepared to fight if needed. Sam's door was still closed.

She could hear unfamiliar voices coming from down the hall. Payton tiptoed down the darkened hall, the hair on the back of her neck standing up. Clinging to the hallway walls as she went, she tried to hear where the voices were coming from. She held her breath as they got louder. The wailing of the alarm was relentless.

Her pulse raced as she glanced around the hall. *Where is Sam?* As Payton crept to the end of the hall, she gasped when she saw the TV on, with the volume blaring.

Suddenly, she felt a hand on her shoulder. Payton let out a yelp and automatically twisted her body to deliver a hard punch. Her right hook smashed against Sam's rock-hard abdomen, winding him.

"Oof... It's me," he wheezed.

She was about to apologize when Sam put a finger to his lips. He motioned for her to stay where she was. He pointed at the front door where the panel to the alarm was located. Payton nodded, rubbing her sore knuckles. He looked back and forth around the living room, finally reaching for the TV remote.

Shutting off the TV, he marched to the alarm panel and entered the code to shut off the deafening alarm. Payton was shaking from the adrenaline rush and being woken so suddenly. She walked over to Sam and stood close to him. In a soft voice, she asked, "What happened to you?"

He touched her upper arm. "I'm sorry, I don't know why I didn't wake sooner," he apologized. "I must have been dead asleep. I didn't realize the alarm was going off until my phone rang next to me. The alarm company is sending the police." He stepped back from Payton, and she immediately felt chilled.

She stood, rubbing her arms. "Why haven't Mark and Alex come to see what's happened?"

Sam rubbed the nape of his neck. "I don't know. I'll check outside in a minute... I'm going to turn on some lights." Sam started by turning on the outside light and the hall light. Soon, there was a knock at the door. Sam peered through the window of the front door. "It's Mark and Alex," he said, flitting his eyes to Payton.

"I'm glad they're okay. I'll wait in the kitchen," said Payton, leaving Sam to deal with the Agents that had been watching the house.

PAYTON GOT HERSELF a glass of water and sat on a stool, pushing her hair out of her face. She was feeling a little better by the time Sam entered the kitchen.

He stood, scratching his head. "Mark and Alex have walked around the outside perimeter. They said it looked like someone's been walking around, but they didn't see anyone approach the house, so they couldn't identify the person. Whoever it was must have tried the door. That would have set off the alarm. There is no one out there now. Are you okay?"

Payton put her arms around herself as her body tensed. She stood and gazed at Sam. "How did the TV get turned on?"

Sam strolled over to Payton and wrapped her in an unexpected hug. All the tension in her body melted away. As he continued to hug her, he explained what he thought had happened. "He must have done it from the window somehow. The front window faces the TV. It would be easy to do." Sam dropped his arms to his side and tilted his head down to look at Payton. She could feel the heat radiating from his body. The intensity of his emotions at that moment took her breath away.

Sam took a step back. "I'm really sorry I didn't wake up right away," he said, frowning.

"It surprised me you weren't up as soon as the alarm went off, with your sensitive hearing and all. Maybe the lack of sleep is catching up with you?" Payton shot him an uneasy smile. She remembered him telling her he had the house alarm installed just in case he didn't wake right away if there was an intruder. This time, the alarm had possibly frightened Brian off, and Payton was grateful for that. She hoped her presence at Sam's home would not bring danger to him. Her stomach clenched at the thought of Brian or any intruder getting inside the house.

Sam scratched his head and yawned. "I'm a heavy sleeper sometimes. Don't worry about me not getting enough rest. I'll manage." He grinned, then glanced at the clock before moving his eyes to Payton's. "It's three a.m. do you want to get more sleep?"

Payton shuddered. "I don't think I can sleep at the moment. The thoughts of someone outside the house... bothers the hell out of me."

Sam put his hands on Payton's upper arms and rubbed up and down. "I hear you. Would it help if you slept in my room?"

He clearly hadn't thought his question through because, seconds after making the offer, Payton could hear his thoughts whirling around in panic. He dropped his hands to his sides and took another step back.

She put a hand up. Her mouth quirked to the side. "It's okay, Sam. If it's all the same with you. I think I'll just sit up with the lights on and read a book. You should try to get some sleep, though."

Sam looked at the ground. His face flushed when he glimpsed Payton once more. "I didn't mean... literally... sleep with me," Sam stammered.

"I know. I can read minds, remember?" Payton tapped her temple.

Sam's pupils flared, and Payton watched as his Adam's apple bobbed up and down. "Don't worry. I don't make it a habit to listen to your every thought. I'm on alert because of what happened tonight," Payton reassured. "I don't think there's any point in me keeping you up all night, too. I need little sleep. I'll be fine."

"Too late. I'm staying up as long as you are." He pulled out a stool to sit next to Payton.

After several minutes of silence, Payton inclined her head to get a better look at Sam. In a soft voice, she asked, "Can I ask you something?"

Sam leaned his folded arms onto the counter and looked at her with a slight crease in his brow. "Sure. What is it?"

"I sensed something today... between you and that female police officer."

Sam nodded and pursed his lips. "Pam? Yeah, we went out twice. I'm sorry I didn't tell you earlier."

Payton waved her hands. "No. That's not what I mean. I got the feeling there was something more going on there. Am I right? You can tell me to mind my business if it's too personal of a question."

Sam sat up straight, splaying his hand's palm down on the counter. He drew a long breath, then blew it out. "It's fine. I don't mind you asking. She was the woman I told you about... she couldn't deal with me being a shifter. It freaked her out."

"What happened? I mean... How long did you see one another?" Payton was too nosy, and she knew it. She was glad Sam didn't seem to mind the questions.

"We went out a handful of times over about a month. It ended before it began, really. After that, I decided it was better to remain single." He shrugged, looking down at his hands.

Payton could see Pam's treatment of him still wounded Sam. She lifted her chin as she spoke. "Well, it's her loss. You deserve better than that." She reached out and patted the top of Sam's hand. He unexpectedly twisted his hand, taking hers and smoothing his thumb alongside it. Payton's breath caught.

"You have nothing to worry about, you know," Sam said with a sexy grin.

She pulled her hand away as if he'd burned it and sat back. "Who says I was worried?" Payton said, feeling defensive. How could he know she was feeling jealous of not just Pam but also Doctor James? She nibbled on her bottom lip, ashamed at her response.

Sam observed her with a knowing look. "I just meant... Look... You are my best friend. I didn't mean to imply anything else. I'm not interested in other women, that's all." His eyes blazed with emotions that Payton wasn't sure she was ready or able to accept.

Despite that, she could barely conceal her delight at his admission. She lowered her head but could feel Sam's eyes on her. Payton tried to ignore the butterflies swirling in her stomach as she looked back at him.

Sam looked flustered and a little hurt. "I'm sorry if I upset things...by taking your hand and saying what I said."

Payton scrunched up her face, feeling guilty. "You didn't. It... You took me by surprise. I'm sorry... I think maybe we should," she began.

Sam's cell phone rang. They both glanced at it before he picked it up off the counter. His forehead furrowed. "I think it's the same caller as before."

Payton reached for the phone before Sam had a chance to answer it.

"Who is this?" she yelled into the phone. Putting it on speaker so that Sam could hear, they both listened to the male voice whisper, "I'm coming for you, Payton."

Payton felt a cold chill. "I dare you to try!" she fumed.

"We are going to find you," Sam yelled into the phone.

"Payton will see me soon enough. But your days are numbered, Sam. See you soon." The call disconnected.

Payton stood and paced. "It looks like your plan is working. Brian knows where you live," Payton mumbled, hugging herself. Unfortunately, that fact did little to reassure her they would catch him.

Sam stood, pushing his stool under the counter. Facing Payton, he raked his fingers through his hair. "There is no way he will get inside the house without us knowing it."

Payton gave a mirthless laugh. "I wish that made me feel better. I don't have a good feeling about Brian and what he has planned."

"I won't let him get to you," Sam reassured, placing a hand at her elbow, stopping her from pacing.

Payton stiffened. Her mind was flooded with thoughts of Brian's threatening notes and phone calls. "It's not me I'm worried about. He keeps threatening to hurt you." She welled up. "What if he goes after *you* to get to me? I couldn't bear it if he" she sniffed, unable to bring herself to finish the sentence.

Sam moved his hand to her shoulder. "He won't get the chance to hurt either of us. I promise you that."

CHAPTER FIVE

PAYTON AND SAM REPORTED to The Agency HQ a lot earlier than usual the following morning. They went straight to the cafeteria and had a light breakfast and coffee while waiting for Frank to arrive at work.

Payton looked around for anyone who appeared suspicious but saw nothing out of the ordinary. Glancing back at Sam, she saw him rubbing his eyes. "I'm sorry that you aren't getting much sleep because of me being at your house."

His face brightened. "I am happy you are staying with me. These things that keep happening are out of your control. Don't worry, I'm fine."

Payton put her elbow on the table and a hand under her chin. "Still... I could think of better ways to keep you awake at night," she teased, then berated herself for not thinking before she spoke.

Sam looked down at the table without saying a word. Payton didn't have to read his thoughts. They were written all over his face.

She squirmed, taking a sip of her coffee.

WHEN SAM AND PAYTON poked their heads into Frank's office, he looked happy to see them. "Good morning. Come on in, you two." He motioned with one hand to wave them in. Sam closed the door behind them as they each took a seat. "How did things go last night?"

Payton rolled her eyes. "After last night, I'm not sure I am going to sleep again until they catch this guy."

Frank's brow creased. "What happened?"

Sam quickly explained what had happened the night before. When he finished, he and Payton exchanged knowing glances before looking back at Frank.

"Brian called about an hour after setting off the house alarm," said Payton.

Frank leaned forward in his chair. "Did anyone see him there?"

Payton shook her head.

"There was no one outside by the time the guys checked, boss. He didn't stick around once the alarm went off," Sam complained.

Frank looked stern. "I don't like the sound of this. Do we know for sure that it is Brian?"

Both Sam and Payton nodded. "It's the same voice on all the phone calls. It's definitely him," said Payton.

"We can't take any chances with him getting near you. I want you to take Bryce back with you tonight. He has offered to stand guard from inside the house," said Frank.

Payton looked over at Sam for reassurance.

"I was the one that brought Bryce on board. We can trust him. He's been heading the Operations Centre for a while now. He's a good guy." Sam smiled warmly.

Payton agreed to have Bryce accompany them. "I'm sorry to be using company resources. I never meant to cause all this drama."

Frank gestured with his hand. "It isn't your fault. You didn't cause any of this. I think that there's something more going on here. Only time will tell whether Lucius is ultimately behind what has been happening. We just need to monitor you until Brian is caught." He paused, and his brows went up. "Joshua has been asking about you as well. Maybe you could go talk to him today?" Frank suggested.

A pang of guilt ran through Payton. Her mind had been focused on other things, and she had neglected her father. Their relationship was still very new, and Payton didn't want to alienate her only family. She looked over at Sam with her brows raised.

"I'll go with you if you like?" he offered.

Payton was glad to have Sam accompany her. The last conversation with Joshua and Azrael had not gone well. Since learning about her part in the prophecy, she wasn't sure how she felt about being an Immortal Guardian. Somehow, being around Sam reminded her that there was more to her than her abilities as an Immortal Witch Guardian.

JOSHUA BEAMED AS PAYTON entered the room, with Sam following close behind her.

Joshua got up from his chair and approached her. "I was hoping you would come to see me." They exchanged a brief hug.

After everyone took a seat, Joshua asked, "Where have you been? Azrael and I were worried about you after our last conversation?"

Payton huffed out some air and tucked some hair behind her ears. "I needed time to get my head around everything. I still can't believe this whole prophecy thing. Frank told me that Azrael left The Agency? Where did he go?"

Joshua's head dropped. When he looked back at Payton, he seemed troubled. "He's gone to retrieve the sword," he said in a low voice.

"What?" she gasped. "Where did Azrael go to retrieve it?"

Joshua looked Payton in the eye. "Not even I know that. He has not shared the location of the sword with anyone. He said to expect his return within about a week."

Payton clucked. "I don't know why he bothered leaving. I told you both that I won't use the sword. There has to be another option to stopping Lucius!" Payton pushed her shoulders back and studied Joshua, wishing they could simply be father and daughter instead of ... well, whatever this was.

His face was stern, but his eyes revealed a tenderness that Azrael's eyes did not. Payton wondered if he, too, was struggling knowing that she was part of a prophecy that included using a magic sword and potentially turning evil because of it?

"As much as I hate to say this, I must. This task is not something you can refuse, Payton. It is your destiny." Joshua's mouth was set in a hard line.

Payton closed her eyes and took a breath before letting out a great sigh. "You don't understand... I can't use the sword! The power inside me is too strong... I'm scared I will take innocent lives. I can't control my emotions the way you and Azrael do. I have actual feelings." She immediately regretted the last thing she said and wished she could take it back.

Joshua tilted his head, a look of hurt clear on his face. "Do not mistake our conduct as us being without emotion. We have feelings. We, too, experience love and anger, just as you do. The difference is we have had millennia to learn how to deal with these emotions. Azrael and I were born with the power that comes from being an Immortal. I know it is not the same for you and requires some time to adjust. Have you been doing the techniques I suggested?"

Payton sighed. "Yes, but it makes no difference. I'm not cut out for this. I can't stop my temper from rising when I am pushed... My inner power is too strong. I can't handle being Immortal."

Joshua's voice was soft. "Give it time."

Tears threatened as her voice caught. "I hate having this prophecy hanging over me. I don't want to kill anyone else! I certainly don't want to go dark by using the sword. I can't wield it. I won't risk it." Payton could only shake her head as she bit her lip.

Sam cleared his throat and spoke up on her behalf. "Someone has been threatening Payton. She has a stalker, and he shows no sign of stopping."

Joshua looked at Payton, alarmed. "Are you okay? Maybe you should stay here in the staff accommodations?"

"She is staying at my house until we find the guy," Sam admitted, looking over at Payton with a look of uncertainty.

Joshua looked relieved. Payton knew Sam would do his best to help keep her safe. Still, she didn't think any of this was fair to her *or* Sam. *It really shouldn't be up to Sam to keep me safe.* She grimaced, putting her hands together in her lap.

Looking at Joshua, her throat suddenly went dry. She swallowed to moisten it before adding, "there's more. I'm having nightmares."

"Nightmares?" Joshua repeated, his eyes widening.

Feeling defensive but unsure why, she snapped, "yeah. Go figure... this Immortal Guardian needs sleep."

Joshua looked disappointed by her reaction, but his voice remained calm. "I did not mean it like that. Believe it or not, I am on your side. I only just found out about you; I do not wish to lose you. You may find it hard to believe, but I care a great deal about what happens to you. For what it is worth, I love you, Payton. You are blood of my blood."

The admission that her father loved her made her well up again. A lump formed in her throat, threatening to choke her. She brushed away another tear.

Joshua looked haunted by her mention of the dreams. "Tell me about these nightmares?"

She sniffed. "I was surrounded by dead bodies and bones of those that the sword turned to ash. I was holding a bloodied sword. That can only mean one thing... can't it?" Payton crinkled her nose, desperately wanting reassurance that she was not in danger of turning evil.

Joshua shook his head, maintaining eye contact with her. "Not necessarily. Your mind could be showing you your worst fear."

Payton put her hand to her forehead. "I don't know. This feels bad... What if?" she couldn't finish. The idea that she could become like Lucius terrified her. It seemed like no one understood her concern. "What happens if I do...you know, become a Fallen One? What would become of me?" she asked, pressing a hand to her jaw, rubbing back and forth anxiously.

Without hesitation, Joshua went to her. Kneeling in front of Payton, he placed his hands on each side of her head. Looking into her eyes, she noticed his own eyes blazed with emotion.

"I will *never* let Lucius or the sword take you. Do you understand? I will die before I allow that to happen." Joshua's eyes burned into hers. She could feel the sincerity in what he was telling her, as emotions of love threatened to overwhelm her. Not since her mother had she felt so much love.

She bit down hard on her lip and spread her arms wide, hugging her father tight. Joshua murmured in her ear. "You are not alone in this. Sam and I are here to help you in any way we can."

As Payton pulled back from the embrace, she could see the intense emotion on Sam's face from across the room. Her heart dared to hope that things would work out okay.

"How did I get so lucky?" She smiled.

She closed her teary eyes, thanking the universe that she had such incredible men in her life. It didn't take away from the fact that she had a destiny to fulfil, but it made her feel less alone.

Now she just had to hope that if she used the sword of power, it would not destroy her or lead her into darkness.

CHAPTER SIX

THE OFFICE WAS QUIET, with Mark and Alex taking the day off. The other two Agents weren't around as was usual. The two female Agents barely spent any time at their desks, and Payton rarely saw them.

Sam had already spoken to Bryce and confirmed that he was still okay to spend the night. It surprised Payton to learn that Bryce was also a shifter, like Sam.

He was a quiet guy with honey-coloured eyes that matched his hair colour. Payton wondered what type of shifter Bryce was but didn't like to ask. She assumed he wasn't a bear shifter since he was slimmer than Sam. Though she realized that body type didn't necessarily indicate that *he wasn't* a bear shifter.

Payton was doing some work at her desk when Sam's phone rang. She was hesitant to answer at first but knew it could be Frank. She stood and stepped to Sam's desk to pick up the phone. "Hello. Sam's phone." She grinned, realizing that Frank didn't need to be told that it was Sam's phone.

"It's Frank. There's been another murder."

"Who is it this time?"

"A witch. I do not have her name," Frank explained before giving Payton the rest of the details.

Sam entered the office carrying two cups of coffee just as Payton was about to go find him. "Frank just called. There's been another murder," she said to Sam.

THE CRIME SCENE YIELDED more than the other supernatural cases had so far. The Sylvan Falls Police were on-site, keeping the public pushed back from the crime scene.

Payton noticed a woman was sitting in the back of one of the police cruisers. As she and Sam approached, Payton grabbed Sam's arm. "That's her. That's the woman I saw in my vision at the murder scene in the alley."

Payton pointed at the woman, who was staring back at her with narrowed eyes.

Sam had taken Payton to a crime scene after they became work partners. There, she'd had a vision of the female suspect who had helped a man commit the murder.

"Are you sure?" Sam asked, glancing at the woman in the car, then back at Payton.

Payton nodded and moved toward the nearest police officer. "Is she the one being blamed for the murder?" She pointed toward the woman in the police car.

The police officer gave them a quick glance before going back to pushing back the crowd that had gathered. He looked as though Payton and Sam were putting him out.

"We're with The Agency," Sam told the man.

The officer pointed to the blue tarp on the ground. "There's your victim."

Payton strolled over and lifted the tarp to see a woman in her late twenties. Her throat was cut. Payton dropped the blue cover and stood.

Although the scene was grisly, Payton sensed the unsuspecting murder victim had died within minutes of the attack.

"Any witnesses?" Sam asked the officer curtly.

"Two. Over there." The officer pointed to two young women huddled together a few feet away.

Payton wasn't sure if the officer was new to Sylvan Falls PD or just didn't want to be there. She could see that Sam didn't like the man's attitude, either. Judging by the police officer's lack of communication, he wasn't crazy about having to tend to a case that wasn't theirs.

Sam and Payton shared a glance before going over to talk to the women. Payton sensed the two women were witches.

After getting their names, Sam asked for details of what they had seen.

"We don't know Maria very well. She didn't run in the same circles as us," one woman stated.

Sam pursed his lips and studied the witnesses. "Did you actually witness the murder take place?"

The women shook their heads. "We saw that woman hurrying out of the alley, and then we noticed Maria on the ground." The witness pointed at the suspect in the police vehicle. Sam nodded.

Payton noted the women's contact details.

"We'll be in touch," Sam muttered as the Agents turned and headed to the police cruiser.

The windows were down in the car's front, and Sam leaned in to speak to the officer sitting inside. "Do you mind bringing her to the station? My partner and I would like to speak with her."

AT SYLVAN FALLS POLICE Department, Payton and Sam observed the murder suspect through the one-way mirror in the tiny observation room.

The suspect, so far unidentified, sat in one of the interrogation rooms next door.

The black-haired woman stared down at the table, motionless. Payton tuned in to the suspect's energy and noted the woman did not seem afraid.

Payton was pleased with the prospect of finally solving a murder case. She knew more killers still needed to be caught and hoped they would learn more about other suspects from the woman they had in custody.

"Do you get a sense she's supernatural? Because I don't." Sam peered at Payton with one brow raised.

"No. I don't," said Payton, putting her hands on her hips. "I also don't think she's going to be very forthcoming."

"What makes you say that?" Sam asked, glancing back at the suspect.

Payton's mouth twisted. "Look at her. She isn't afraid. She's acting like she's waiting for her coffee order."

Sam let out a laugh. "Well, let's see if that cool demeanour sticks around once we chat."

Payton snickered, and the pair went to speak to their suspect.

The woman made a wry face as Payton and Sam took seats across from her.

"What is your name?" asked Payton.

The woman glared at Payton without responding.

Sam sighed. "Fine. What were you doing at the scene of a murder?"

The woman leaned her elbows on the table, clasping her handcuffed hands in front of her. "I do not know what you are talking about."

"I'll ask you again. What's your name?" Payton's tone was more authoritative this time.

"What is it to you? I did nothing wrong." The woman squinted at Payton.

Sam sat back in his chair. "We have identified you from another crime scene. You and a male suspect murdered a woman almost a month ago," he accused.

The woman shrugged and fixed her eyes on Sam. "I do not know what you are talking about."

Payton could tell that Sam's accusation surprised the woman. The suspect obviously thought they had gotten away with their crime. Feeling as though there was more going on beneath the surface, she tried a different tactic. "Do you work for Lucius?" A brief flash of recognition showed on the suspect's face.

I knew it. Payton felt confident that they were going to get somewhere at last. She just had to get the woman to open up.

"How did you come to be in the alley today?" Sam asked.

The suspect rolled her eyes at Sam. "Who says I was there?" she crowed.

Payton tuned in to the woman's aura to see that it was yellow with pockets of dark red and streaks of grey. *That's odd*?

She listened to the woman's thoughts for anything that might be helpful. The suspect moved her eyes to Payton's while her lips curled into a devious grin. Reaching her hands to tap the side of her head, she jeered, "trying to find something?"

Payton was taken aback. "Are you a telepath?" she blurted. Payton adjusted herself in her chair and decided the woman was only guessing and not a telepath herself. *Maybe she felt me inside her head? But how?*

The suspect didn't respond, which only convinced Payton further that she was on the right track. With determination, she probed deeper into the woman's mind. Flashes of words sprung up, but it was evident that the woman knew how to hide her thoughts just as Payton did.

Puzzled, Payton pushed further. Her confidence increased. She'd never thought of using her abilities to probe the minds of suspects before. *This could work.*

The suspect fixed her eyes on Payton's. "I can feel you inside my head. Stop it!" she snapped.

Payton could feel Sam's eyes on her, but she refused to look at him. She sensed he might disapprove of her method of getting information. Something about the woman felt off, and Payton was growing impatient with the tiny bits of information the woman's mind was revealing. She felt her jaw tighten. "Are you a human?" Payton asked. She wasn't picking up any supernatural vibe from the woman, but something was definitely odd about her.

After more silence, Payton smacked her palms hard on the table, startling the woman. In her periphery, she caught sight of Sam's head flying back in surprise.

"Where the hell is Lucius? I know you know him!" Payton felt the rise of power inside her and feebly pushed back at it. Part of her wanted to scare the woman, hoping that she would give up whatever information she was hiding.

Payton slammed her hands back down on the table again, causing it to vibrate this time. The lights in the room flickered as Payton's ancient power nudged at her to be freed.

Instead of looking afraid, the woman looked smug.

Payton swallowed hard as her frustration mounted. It took everything inside her not to reach across the table and throttle her.

Sam reached out and touched Payton's hand that was on the table. She jerked it away. "This woman knows something. I know she does," Payton snapped without looking in Sam's direction.

She put her hands back on the table and leaned toward the suspect. "Who killed that woman today?"

The suspect shrugged.

"You may as well tell us. You'll be going to jail for murder one way or another. We charge you with murdering at least one supernatural being. Maybe two," Sam threatened.

"Oh? We'll see about that," she scoffed.

Payton glowered. The table and chairs were shifting as though a minor earthquake was rolling through the room. At last, she noted an almost imperceptible glimpse of fear on the woman's face. She felt pretty sure Sam wasn't too happy with the display, either.

Payton pointed at the murder suspect. "Here's what I think. I think you are a servant or colleague of the Fallen Immortal, Lucius. Also known as the master! I believe he has you and others like you killing supernaturals... what I don't know is why?"

The woman scrutinized Payton for a moment. "Others like me? Humph... Good theory. Have any more stories for me?" the suspect mocked.

Payton stood up straight, thrusting her shoulders back. She probed the woman's mind again. This time, she pushed harder. The woman flinched as if in pain.

Payton continued to press, looking for anything that could link the woman to Lucius. Finally, a name flashed briefly, and Payton caught it.

Grinning, Payton asked, "Nadia? Is that your name?"

The woman sneered in response.

Payton studied her without blinking. "Okay, Nadia. Where is Lucius?"

When there was no verbal response, she probed the woman's mind again.

Sam sat in silence next to Payton. She could feel his disapproval but didn't care what he thought of her interrogation techniques. She knew Lucius was behind the murders, and she was determined to stop him and any more murders from occurring.

She continued to push and explore Nadia's mind until she felt the barriers breaking down at last.

Just a little more.

At last, she got a glimpse of a man's face. The man with the piercing brown eyes. *Lucius!*

The woman cried out in pain. "Stop. I cannot take it. You are hurting me..." Her nose bled. She wiped at it with her cuffed hands while making an angry face at the Agents.

Payton released the hold on the woman's mind. The room calmed, and the lights stopped flickering as Payton quashed her inner power. She sat back down in her chair, feeling rather proud of herself. And she did it all without destroying the room.

I'm getting better at this stuff, she told herself.

Sam moved to reach for a box of tissue at the end of the table. He handed it to Nadia. Payton finally met Sam's gaze. He looked at her as if asking, *'What the hell was that?'*

"I went looking for Lucius, and I found him," she spoke aloud, thrusting her chin out. "She knows where he is."

Nadia's head was tilted back, and she was holding a tissue to her nose.

"What now?" Sam muttered as he continued to gawk at Payton in surprise. She could see he was feeling uncomfortable.

Nadia viewed Payton, clearly distressed. "I will talk if you stop with the mind-probing."

Payton folded her arms across her chest. A minute passed before Nadia spoke, "what do you want to know?"

Payton focused all of her attention on Nadia. "I want to know where Lucius is? Why is he doing all this?"

Nadia looked Payton in the eye. "He has a handful of people at his side. I am not one of them... The murders are intended to scare the humans out of Sylvan Falls," she explained.

Sam huffed, shaking his head. "Why? What is the point of scaring humans into leaving town?"

"I do not know. What difference does it make? Next question?" Nadia pressed her lips in defiance.

"What is his end game?" asked Payton, hoping to gain insight into how she might stop Lucius. She had a feeling Nadia was lying about what she knew. Still, Payton figured any information at this point was better than none.

Nadia rolled her eyes. "I am unaware of what Lucius's ultimate plan is."

Sam and Payton looked skeptically at one another and back at Nadia.

"Is he trying to start a war between the various supernaturals? Are there supernaturals working with Lucius?" Sam demanded.

Nadia dropped her head and gave a long sigh. "Look. I thought you wanted to know if I killed someone? What's with all the questions about Lucius?"

With her patience thoroughly tested, Payton probed Nadia's mind once more.

Nadia squirmed, then looked up at her and blinked. "We are done here."

"Tell me where Lucius is hiding?" barked Payton.

Nadia's shoulders slumped. "I said we are done," she hissed through caged teeth.

Sam shook his head and glanced at Payton. "Can I see you outside for a minute?" He got up from his seat, putting his hand on Payton's shoulder.

The pair stepped out into the hallway.

Sam turned to Payton with a look of annoyance. "I don't know what you think you're doing in there, but it isn't helping."

"I saw Lucius in her mind. She knows where he is, Sam," Payton said defensively.

"Look, I get that you want to find Lucius and deal with him once and for all. But we have a murder to solve today, and we need her to talk. Whatever you are doing to her is not helping," Sam argued.

Payton put her arms out to the side. "We both know she killed someone... if not the woman today, then another one. I saw her in my vision. Can't we just arrest her and interrogate her after she has had some time in a cell?"

Sam's expression was stern. "We will arrest her, but we also need to do a proper investigation here. Torture is not what we do at The Agency." He grimaced.

Payton clenched her fists at her side. "Who says I am torturing her?"

Sam rolled his eyes but didn't respond.

Payton continued, "you and I both know there is more going on here than meets the eye. We need to catch Lucius so we can put an end to this once and for all. I want to find out what's really going on, and I believe she knows." She put her hand on the doorknob of the interrogation room, preparing to go back in.

Sam reached out and gently grasped her elbow.

Payton turned her head to look at him.

He frowned but looked less annoyed and more worried this time. "One other thing...." he looked Payton in the eyes. "If this woman isn't human, and she's not supernatural, what is she?"

Payton's eyes bulged. She smacked her palm to her forehead. "Crap. Of course. Why didn't I realize it?" she exclaimed, quickly pulling the door open.

They both stepped back into the room to see Nadia standing next to the table, holding her broken handcuffs. She dropped them to the floor. "I almost had you," the woman spat, glaring at Payton.

The Agents stood blocking the room's only exit. Payton put her hands out to her side. "Why did you let the police arrest you? Why sit in the cruiser waiting? You could have taken off at any time." Payton was confused. Did she want to be arrested?

Nadia laughed. "How do you know I didn't want to be arrested?" she taunted.

Payton studied the woman. "Why would you want that?"

Nadia shrugged. "I needed to see *you* for myself."

Payton and Sam shared a brief, worried look.

Nadia gave a dirty look to Payton and curled her lips into a sneer. She suddenly took a running leap at Payton, reaching for her throat.

Payton blocked the woman's reach, shoving her arm away.

"I don't think so." Payton managed as she continued to tussle with the woman, blocking her each time she reached for Payton.

Without hesitation, Sam blurted, "I've got you." He grabbed Nadia's arms from behind while Payton fended off the Fallen Immortal. Payton swept the woman's legs out from under her with one foot, causing Nadia to stumble against Sam. They wrestled her to the floor.

Nadia was no match for both Sam and Payton, even with her own inhuman strength. Payton knelt and pressed the woman's body to the floor with one hand, almost sitting on top of her.

Sam maintained a hold of Nadia's arms as he knelt on the floor.

Placing one hand on the woman's chest, Payton snapped, "we need to search her pockets. She has an enchanted medallion with her. It's what prevented me from knowing she's Immortal."

Nadia's face distorted in frustration, and she kicked her legs to knock Payton off of her. Payton straddled Nadia and looked at Sam.

He tilted his head. "I'll hold her while you search?"

Payton obliged and rifled through the woman's pockets, quickly finding the enchanted medallion.

She shoved the large coin into her own pocket for safekeeping. Payton heard a faint ringing in her ears telling her Nadia was indeed a Fallen One.

She narrowed her eyes at the woman. "Nice try," said Payton.

Nadia rolled her eyes. "What are you going to do? Kill me? Payton?"

Payton bristled. The Fallen One knew her name? Neither she nor Sam had introduced themselves to her.

"Tell us where the rest of the Fallen Immortals are?" Payton demanded.

Nadia closed her eyes for a moment. "Let me up."

Payton glared at her. "Will you keep your hands to yourself?"

Nadia nodded, closing and opening her eyes slowly.

Sam stood, releasing her arms and running his hands through his hair. "I don't think we're going to get much more out of her. Let's just lock her up."

Payton agreed. They needed to make sure she didn't get back to Lucius. "Call Frank. Ask him to bring unbreakable restraints. If The Agency has such a thing for Immortals?"

Sam nodded and left the room.

Payton stretched out her hand to assist Nadia to stand. Then stood back, eyeing her. She knew they were probably evenly matched in terms of strength, and magic would do nothing to help her against another Immortal. Even a Fallen One. It made little sense that Nadia was here. Why would she want to be in custody? What did she have to gain by being locked up?

"Sit down," Payton ordered, pointing toward the chair.

Nadia stayed where she was and crossed her arms, looking Payton up and down. "Finally, I meet the great Payton Adams," she trumpeted.

Payton didn't respond. Her brow creased.

Nadia continued, "Lucius has a real thing for you."

Payton snorted and rolled her eyes. "Sure he does."

"No. Really. Lucius says, you are something special," Nadia sized up Payton for a second time with a sour expression. "I do not know what all the fuss is about."

Payton ignored her comment. "Why have you allowed yourself to be caught?"

Nadia shrugged, keeping her eyes on Payton.

"How many Fallen Immortals are working with Lucius?" Payton persisted.

"I am sure all will be revealed soon enough," Nadia retorted.

Payton's lip curled. "You let yourself be manipulated by Lucius. Why? What do you get out of all this?"

"Who says he manipulated me?" Nadia scorned.

Highly skeptical, Payton asked, "I suppose you're going to tell me Lucius does not know what you've done, getting yourself arrested?"

"He will now, I'm sure." Nadia glared.

Payton tried one more time, knowing it was probably futile. "Stop playing games. Tell me where Lucius is hiding?"

Nadia leaned forward with a spiteful expression on her face. "No."

"Is he the reason you know who I am?" asked Payton, folding her arms.

"Does that matter?" Nadia had a sinister grin.

Payton crinkled her nose. For the first time since meeting Nadia, she felt unsure of what to say. "Of course it does. I want to know what Lucius knows about me?"

Was he watching her? Was he the reason Brian was stalking her? She felt a chill snake up and down her spine.

Nadia was studying her. "He knows enough. I know he will not give up until he has you at his side. You're the reason he moved forward with his plans." She smirked.

Payton's eyes widened. She took a step back. Was he going to try to turn her into a Fallen One? "Are you saying I'm the reason for all the murders?" *But why?*

Nadia laughed maniacally. "Don't act so innocent. You had to know that he would do something to get your attention."

She stiffened. "I don't even know Lucius, and I don't want his attention." Payton's voice came out more high-pitched than she intended. "I certainly don't want to join him." Payton felt sick to her stomach. "He is killing innocent people. I would not do that. Nor do I condone it."

Nadia snorted. "Oh, please. Now, who is lying? Let me ask you something? How did it make you feel?"

Panic coursed through Payton. Did Nadia know about the lives she'd already taken? She gulped. "How did *what* make me feel?"

Nadia's eye's darkened. "Killing the necromancer?"

Payton felt a mix of dread and fury. *No.* How did Nadia know so much about her?

Sam re-entered the interview room. "Frank is on his way," he said, glancing over at Payton. His brows knitted at the sight of her. Payton pressed her lips and gave a subtle shake of her head.

Sam turned to look at Nadia. "Are you sure you don't want to tell us more about your accomplice in the murder or murders?"

She let out a laugh. "Not a chance."

"It's no use. The Fallen One would rather be locked up," grunted Payton, wanting to get out of the room and far away. The Fallen Immortals revelations about Lucius had her more wound up than ever. Was she really the reason for all the trouble in Sylvan Falls? She shook her head as bile rose in her throat. *Please, God, no.* Payton paced back and forth.

It wasn't long before there was a knock on the door, and Frank entered the room with Joshua in tow. Payton's body tensed. She looked over at Nadia as Frank and Sam put unique cuffs around her wrists that she presumably could not break.

Payton let out a relieved breath. It looked as though Azrael told the truth about one thing. The Fallen could not sense Immortal Guardians. Thankfully, Nadia also didn't seem to recognize Joshua as a founder of Sylvan Falls.

Sam and Frank led Nadia out of the room.

Payton's eyes widened, and she sent a telepathic question to Joshua. *'Do you know who she is?'*

Joshua stepped up to Payton. "I do not know who she is. It is possible that she was part of the second wave of Immortals that came over from our world. I do not know all Immortals personally. What did she tell you?" Joshua asked.

"She said that Lucius knows about me. In fact, *she* knew who I was. You don't think they have been spying on me, do you?" Payton was reluctant to admit everything Nadia had told her. At least not yet.

Joshua looked perplexed. "It is possible. Although it is unclear why he would do that."

Payton bit her bottom lip for a moment, then said, "I think I know why. Nadia told me I am the reason Lucius is having supernaturals killed." She shuddered.

Joshua's face creased with worry. He stepped closer to Payton and put a hand on her shoulder, just as Azrael always did.

"It is troubling to know that Lucius is aware of you, I will admit. But you must not take the blame for his actions. None of this is your fault." Joshua frowned. "I hope this does not mean that your stalker is working with him. Please promise me you will be careful?"

CHAPTER SEVEN

PAYTON WAS RELIEVED when Nadia was locked in a secure cell at The Agency even though it was only a temporary holding facility. The large supernatural prison was out of the province in the Yukon Territories. But something told Payton they weren't going to be sending Nadia off anytime soon. They needed more information about Lucius before they shipped her off. At the very least, they wanted to prove that she took part in the murders.

With Nadia locked away, Payton and Sam sat down in Frank's office.

"Good job today," said Frank.

Sam scoffed. "We did nothing. The suspect was already in custody at the scene. We don't even know if she is the one who committed the murder."

Frank pursed his lips. "I am sure she'll change her mind about sharing information when she realizes her only other option is to live in a six by eight-foot cell."

Don't be too sure, Payton thought.

She put her finger up. "I want to have another go at getting Nadia to talk before we do anything else." The fact that Nadia knew who Payton was disturbed her. Who else was Lucius working with? She had to know, and Nadia was the one who could tell her.

Frank looked troubled. "Sam filled me in on your earlier interrogation... Maybe try to be more careful this time?"

Payton screwed up her face and fixed her gaze on Sam. He shrugged with his hands out. "You worried me. You made the woman's nose bleed."

Payton rolled her eyes, shrugging off his comment. "I knew what I was doing. Besides, Nadia's a damned Fallen Immortal. Whatever I do to her isn't going to make a difference to her well-being."

Sam and Frank stared open-mouthed at Payton. She sighed and pushed herself up and out of her chair. "I'm going down to the cells. I'll meet you in Ops, Sam." Payton strolled out of Frank's office without another word.

PAYTON WALKED INTO the short hallway lined with several small prison cells, stopping to peer into Nadia's cell. Nadia was lying back on her bunk with a hand behind her head. Sitting up, Nadia flung her feet over the side of her bed. "Miss me already?"

Payton held the bars of the cell as she watched Nadia. "Hardly. I've come to ask you one more time about Lucius?"

"And I told you, I am done talking with you about him," said Nadia.

Payton dropped her hands at her side. "How did you know who I am, if not from Lucius?"

"All the Fallen Immortals in town know who you are. We've had our eyes on you for a while now." A cruel grin filled her face.

At least she knew she was definitely being watched, not that it did anything to reassure her. "Do you know Brian Thomas?" Payton asked.

Nadia shrugged without responding. The woman seemed strangely calm at having been arrested and locked up. What was she really up to?

Payton stood tall, not wanting to show any more vulnerability than she already had. "What is Lucius's next move?"

Nadia got up and slowly waltzed over to where Payton was standing. She tilted her head towards Payton. "Let me make this easy to understand... He is coming for YOU."

Payton drew back, unable to hide the chill that crept up her spine once more. She spun on her heel and stormed out, going back to operations to join Sam.

One way or another, Payton was going to find Lucius's hiding spot. She had no choice. The violence in town had to be stopped. Especially if she was the reason for the killings. She wondered again if Brian was working with him. The idea that she was part of Lucius's insidious plan made her feel sick to her stomach.

PAYTON WAS UNSETTLED by Nadia's comments, not to mention her reaction toward the woman while interrogating her. Payton knew she wasn't the most patient person, but her methods had been less than kind when it came to probing Nadia's mind. She wasn't proud of her behaviour.

The last thing Payton needed was to give Lucius precisely what he wanted. She had to learn to control the darker side of her Immortality before it was too late, and she hurt someone else.

Payton wondered what Lucius would do if he got his hands on her. What if Lucius and Brian both planned on harming Sam to get to her?

The very thought of Sam being hurt filled Payton with so much anger and sadness that the lights in the hallway flickered. She closed her eyes, pressing her hand up against the wall. The lights stopped blinking.

Regaining her composure, Payton tucked hair behind her ears and smoothed her hands down her sides. Taking a couple of deep breaths, she headed toward the elevator to meet Sam.

When the elevator door opened and Payton stepped out onto the platform in Ops, she saw Sam looking up at her, his face filled with uncertainty. She headed down the stairs and over to him. His expression softened as she approached, and she felt terrible for her earlier treatment of him.

"Did she tell you anything more?" he asked.

Payton shook her head and pulled Sam to one side so they could speak privately. Sam tilted his head as he looked at her.

Payton grimaced. "I'm sorry about the way I treated you today. You were right in being concerned. I should never have interrogated Nadia in that way. Once I knew she was connected to Lucius, I couldn't stop myself." Payton shoved her hands in her pockets. "I know it's no excuse for my behaviour. I will try to do better."

Sam put a hand on her shoulder and stroked it. "I know you have been under a lot of stress, and I put it down to that," he shrugged.

Payton smiled thinly. "Believe me, I want to find the murderers and stop the chaos in town as much as you do. I never expected to be face to face with a Fallen Immortal. Especially one that is working with Lucius. I think you're right, though. With being stalked, learning about the prophecy, the sword, then both of us being threatened and now finding Nadia... I am not feeling very calm about things."

Sam kept his hand on her shoulder as he spoke and took a step closer to her, "you are doing better than you think. Today was not a regular occurrence for you. We'll get them *both*, don't worry." Sam peered around to make sure no one was watching or potentially listening to them. "Do you think Lucius is working with Brian?"

Payton bit her lip. "I think so. Yes."

She felt her body going increasingly warm as Sam continued to maintain physical contact. She turned, pretending to be looking around, forcing Sam to remove his hand.

Sliding her hands to her hips, she whispered. "I just had a thought. Maybe we could ask Margret to help us find Lucius?" Payton raised a brow. "You up for trying?"

Sam nodded and followed Payton to the elevator.

Margret, the supreme witch elder, was the last person Payton wanted to ask for help but likely was the only one that could help them.

THEY REACHED THE SAFE house nearly thirty minutes later.

Payton chuckled. "I bet she's pissed being this far out of town," she said, getting out of the SUV. Things between her and Sam felt good again. She wanted to keep it that way. For that reason, she decided not to tell him that Lucius was having people murdered because of her.

"Margret wanted to be kept safe," Sam laughed. "Besides, I doubt anyone would look for her out here."

Sam knocked on the door, but there was no immediate response. He looked over at Payton. Knowing he was silently asking her to tune in to Margret's energy, she obliged.

Payton motioned with a thumb out, "she's on the other side of the door."

Sam knocked again and announced, "It's Sam and Payton. Let us in."

The door opened, and Margret stared back at them expectantly. "Have you caught Lucius yet?" she asked as the two Agents entered the house, closing the door behind them.

"Not exactly," Payton responded.

"Why are you here if you haven't found him?" Margret snarked.

Payton reached into her pocket and pulled out the enchanted medallion she had taken from Nadia. She held it out to Margret. "Since you created this, I was hoping you could use magic to show us where he's hiding."

Margret picked up the medallion and examined it, then dropped it back into Payton's hand with a look of indignation on her face. "I don't need this to do a location spell if that's what you are asking me? Good heavens, child, can't you even do that?" Margret scolded.

Payton resisted the urge to slap Margret and took a step back to avoid standing so close to the horrid woman. The Supreme Elder was not the most pleasant of people to deal with, making Payton glad she had avoided becoming part of the witch community in Sylvan Falls. Her unique ability to pick up on the emotions of others was always problematic when Margret was around. She hoped that Margret's fear of Lucius would prompt her to help them.

"Can you do it or not?" Sam demanded.

Margret looked peeved. "Of course I can. But it won't be an *exact* location. We can get some idea what part of town he's in. I'll need a few things from my office."

Feeling hopeful, Payton motioned for Margret to follow her outside. "Let's go. The sooner we get this-" she stopped speaking when Margret froze. "I'm not going out there! Don't be so foolish."

Payton saw Sam's face change. He put a finger in Margret's face. "Stop! You will speak to Payton with respect, or I will personally drive you back to your own home. I've had enough of you. Help us so we can find Lucius," Sam scolded.

Payton made no attempt to hide her smile at Sam's outburst. She pulled out a map, opened it, and laid it out on a nearby table. "If you don't want to leave the house, you will have to make do with a map of Sylvan Falls. I'm sure someone as powerful as you can do that?"

Margret snorted. Much to her chagrin, she looked down at the map, then over at the Agents. "Does one of you at least have a lighter?"

"In the car. I'll be right back," Sam said, leaving to get the lighter.

Payton ignored Margret for a moment and looked at the map splayed out on the table. She wondered how the witch elder would do a location spell with just a map of Sylvan Falls and a lighter? Payton hadn't been sure if a map would be of any use in the spell or not but brought it with her, anyway.

It was times like this that she wished she had more experience doing practical magic. Her proficiency was now with battle magic and using the elements to fight when needed.

Doing location spells and other basic elemental magic was not really in her wheelhouse. However, that didn't stop her from trying a magic spell or two once in a while. Being an Immortal Guardian had caused all her abilities to become heightened.

Regrettably, basic magic spells like a location spell were not the sort of magic she had been practicing with since becoming Immortal. Lord knew her mother never wanted her to use any magic at all.

She turned her head to look intently at Margret. "When you met with Lucius, did he ever bring anyone with him? A woman, maybe?"

Margret looked a little disappointed by the question. "No. Lucius always visited me alone."

Payton folded her arms, her brows knitted. "And you're sure you made six medallions and not more?"

Margret opened her mouth to speak. She stopped and bowed her head. Payton guessed she was about to make another snide remark and thought better of it.

She studied Margret's auric field for any changes. "I can't believe you didn't realize he was a Fallen Immortal," Payton chided.

"How would I? I can sense other witches, but I can't tell the difference between humans and anyone else. I wasn't even sure what you were until Lucius told me."

Curious, Payton asked, "what did Lucius tell you about me exactly?"

"He made me believe Immortals were running The Agency and that you are one as well. The idea was he was protecting the town from you... or Immortals."

So he had lied to manipulate Margret. Payton wondered if anything Nadia told her was true. Did Lucius really want her? If so, was it so that he could destroy her? Or was it so that he could turn her?

Payton eyed Margret. "You say he thinks The Agency is run by Immortals. Did he tell you about these other supposed Immortals?"

Margret squinted her eyes as if in thought. "Not specifically. No. Just you."

Payton put a hand on her hip. "It never occurred to you to ask how he knew I was Immortal?"

Margret paused, trying to come up with a response. "Well... he was persuasive," she admitted.

Payton's stomach turned at the idea of what that meant. "Did he tell you about any plans for The Agency or me?" she asked, pushing away the knowledge of Margret's infatuation with Lucius.

A look of guilt crossed the Supreme Elder's face, and Payton wondered what sort of plan she had hatched with Lucius.

"I know he doesn't like The Agency and has plans to destroy it, but I don't know how he plans to do it. I am unaware of his intentions toward you."

Payton could tell the woman was lying but guessed it was because of her own role in whatever he was planning.

"By the way, there has been another murder. A witch this time," Payton stated.

Margret put a hand to her chest. "I... I didn't know." A look of distress crossed her face. Payton wondered if Margret actually felt bad about the murder or if she was just counting her blessings that she hadn't been killed by Lucius and his minions.

Sam came back inside the house and passed the lighter to Margret.

Margret had a look of determination that Payton had not witnessed from her before. The woman smoothed her clothes for a moment, looking ashamed. "I'm sorry to hear there has been another murder. I just want you to know that I will help to stop these demons any way that I can."

"Let's start with finding out where they are hiding for now," said Payton, managing a small smile. Maybe Margret cared about more than just herself, after all? At the very least, she cared about the witches and warlocks under her leadership. *I guess that counts for something,* Payton thought.

Margret stepped up to the map and began an incantation, moving her hands in a circular motion over it. She did this three times and then lit a corner of the map with the lighter.

Payton and Sam watched with curiosity as the map burned. The fire went out on its own, leaving a small piece of the map untouched by the flames.

Payton walked over and picked up the remaining piece of the map and showed it to Sam.

"It's at the Northern edge of town. There are a lot of farms there. It could take a while to find the right one," he said.

Margret was looking at them with a hopeful expression.

Sam smiled. "Thank you for your help."

Margret nodded, putting a trembling hand to her lips.

"Let's take a drive to the edge of town," quipped Payton.

"IT'S NO USE. WE'LL never find Lucius and his group this way," snapped a frustrated Payton.

Sam was taken aback. He peered over at her. "It's not like you to give up so quickly."

Payton's lips twisted. "We've been driving around for over an hour. I don't see or feel anything out of the ordinary. He could be in any of these farmhouses, and we wouldn't know it."

"Look at it this way. At least we have a rough idea where he is. We can tell Frank, and he can send people to check out each farm," said Sam.

Payton rolled her eyes. "Let's head back to HQ." She looked out the window at the fields with mountains far off in the distance. "Why would he stay out here?" she wondered aloud.

"For the same reason, we hid Margret on the other side of town. Few people would expect them to be in those locations," Sam responded. "Have you tried picking anything up from the coin thingy?"

With the way the day had been going, she hadn't stopped to think about it.

"Great idea," she said, pulling the medallion out of her pocket. She held it in her hands and closed her eyes. The first thing she was aware of was the powerful magic that Margret had imbued it with.

Going beyond that, she received flashes of faces. Two of them stood out more than the rest. Her eyes popped open. "I saw a couple of male faces, but no houses or farms. I wonder if the men I saw are other Fallen Immortals?"

BACK AT HQ, PAYTON scrolled through The Agency's watch list of supernaturals trying to find the men from her vision. She put her elbows on the desk and pinched the bridge of her nose. "They must be Immortals. They aren't in the database," she muttered. "So much for getting more information on them." She sighed, throwing her arms out to the side.

"Maybe we should check surveillance footage from town for the day of the warlock murder," Sam suggested.

Payton agreed, and they strolled to Ops to use one of their computers to check it out.

Unfortunately, aside from seeing Lucius talking with the two men, their wide-brimmed hats made it impossible for facial recognition to identify them.

Sitting next to one another, Sam reached over and put a hand on Payton's upper back. "Let's head home for today," he said, loud enough for the other employees in operations to hear him.

Payton stood and leaned her mouth close to Sam's ear. "Do you really think Brian's helper could be in operations?" She looked around to see if anyone was watching them. Several employees turned away as she scanned the people in the room.

"Let's tell Frank we're leaving," said Sam.

Sam knocked on Frank's open door. His boss looked worried as he hung up the phone.

"We are just about to head home," grinned Sam, motioning toward the hall.

Frank motioned for them to step inside the room and close the door. The Agents took a seat.

"The police have gone to Brian's home, but he isn't there. It looks as though he hasn't been home for a while. They will have someone watch the house. When he returns, they will arrest him."

Sam gave a wry smile. "I don't suppose we'd be lucky enough that he left town?"

Frank scratched his forehead. "I doubt it. I just thought you two should know. He may show up at your place tonight but with us outside and Bryce inside with you, I am confident we will catch him."

Payton felt less worried about going to Sam's this time because more people would be watching the place than any other night so far.

Sylvan Falls police would be parked outside, along with Frank and another agent.

Hopefully, they would capture Brian once and for all, putting an end to his threats. Chatting with Sam and Frank about the last few days, Payton shared her concern that Brian, Lucius, and Nadia were somehow connected. She neglected to mention the part about her being to blame for Lucius's plan being enforced. After all, she had no proof that this was the case. *Nadia could be lying*, Payton told herself.

CHAPTER EIGHT

WHEN THEY ARRIVED AT Sam's, they hurried inside, where Sam closed the blinds and curtains to avoid a repeat of the night before. Despite having had the house alarm on all day, he and Bryce did a quick check throughout the house for any sign of trouble.

They had picked up Chinese takeout for dinner, so Payton remained in the kitchen, where she pulled out a couple of plates and cutlery while she waited for the men to join her.

Everyone inside the place had direct contact with Frank and two police officers outside through blue-tooth earpieces. They weren't in the house long before Payton's cell phone rang.

She didn't recognize the number. "Here we go," she muttered, answering the phone. "Hello."

"I told you to stay away from Sam. Why do you continue to defy me?" the male voice snapped.

"Brian, this has to stop." Payton tried to keep her voice even.

"I told you I am coming for you. You will be with me."

"I don't understand why you're doing this?" Payton tensed.

"You can't hide. And you can't run. Sam will die if you continue to avoid me. Come to me, and no one has to get hurt."

"Where are you?" Payton asked. "If you tell me, I will come to you," she lied.

The phone went silent as the caller hung up.

She stared at her phone, wondering where Brian was calling her from.

"Payton?" Sam's voice called out.

She turned her head toward the entrance to the kitchen to see Bryce and Sam watching her.

"What happened?" asked Sam.

"I got call a from Brian. He is angry because I am still around you." Payton's head was spinning. She didn't want to face him alone, but she didn't want Sam to confront him.

Sam reached her within a couple of long strides. "Any clues where he is?"

Payton shook her head.

Sam ran his hand through his hair and bit his lip. "I'm going to go outside and look around the house. Bryce, stay with her." He started out of the room.

"Sam, no! It can't be you. He sees you as a threat," Payton exclaimed.

Sam stopped and observed Payton. "We have to do something!" His jaw flexed. "We need to draw this guy out. You have mind control powers. I've seen you use it. Can't you see if he is in the area and draw him out?"

Payton closed her eyes and focused her psychic senses on locating anyone outside that shouldn't be there. Eventually, she sensed a stranger nearby, and a vision flashed in her mind of a grey sedan parked on the street. Her eyes popped open.

"What? What did you see?" Sam asked, his voice sounding urgent.

Payton's body was suddenly on high alert. He was right outside!

"He's on the street. In a grey sedan."

Bryce ran out of the room, calling out, "I've got this!"

Sam wasn't far behind him.

PAYTON STOOD BY THE front door, peering out at the street. Her stomach was in knots as she watched for any sign of Bryce and Sam. They'd been gone for about ten minutes, and Payton felt concerned they hadn't reported back.

She called out to Frank on her headset when there was no sound coming from Sam or Bryce. "Frank, can you see them?" she implored.

There was a long pause before a winded Frank answered. "I can see Bryce. The car's gone. Sam followed it."

Payton put a hand to her earpiece. "Oh my god. Where is he?"

She was met with silence. "Frank. Where is Sam?"

Frank's alarmed voice echoed in her ear. "I'm sorry. Sam's gone. I don't see him."

"What do you mean, gone?" Payton threw open the front door and ran to the street.

Looking down the street, she saw Bryce standing about thirty feet away on the side of the road, holding his head. Turning to peer in the opposite direction, she saw Frank running toward her, looking alarmed.

Panic rose in her when there was no sign of Sam anywhere.

"Oh my god, this is all my fault," she cried.

Frank reached her, trying to catch his breath, "It's not your fault."

"I told them there was a car outside. I led them right to him!" Payton stood, shaking her head as tears stained her cheeks.

Frank grasped her upper arms. "Listen, we have to act quickly."

Payton found it hard to breathe. Grief and fear were overwhelming her. She attempted to regain her composure, but the feeling of nausea was intense. "What happened?" she cried.

Frank frowned and took Payton's face in his hands. His voice was calm as he looked into her eyes. "A car was parked down the road from where we were parked." He pointed behind him. "It was far enough away that we thought it belonged to the house down the street. Bryce and Sam ran out of the house but didn't get very far before the guy drove off. He hit Bryce with his car as he sped off. Sam chased after him. We've been searching the area for the last ten minutes for Sam."

Payton's mouth fell open in shock.

Frank placed his hands back at his sides.

"Is Bryce okay?" she asked, turning to see blood streaming down one side of his face. Bryce wasn't looking at Payton and talked to the police officer standing with him.

"He hit the ground pretty hard. His head is cut, but I think he should be okay," said Frank.

Payton trembled. She was shocked by the sight of Bryce. "I can heal him," she mumbled as she ran to him in a daze.

Bryce and the police officer were startled as she ran up to them and put her hands on Bryce. "I can heal you," Payton cried, with tears streaming down her cheeks. Bryce winced when she put a hand over the cut without waiting for his response. It closed over and healed within seconds.

"Thanks," said Bryce, looking confused.

Frank called out to her as he caught up to them. His voice was a little more frantic than before. "Payton, Sam isn't anywhere to be found. We need your head to be clear. You will have to help track him."

"Track him? But I..?" Payton was puzzled. She wiped her cheeks with the backs of her hands. Payton couldn't feel Sam. How could she track him?

Bryce interjected, "I can help find Sam."

"Great," said Frank.

The police officer went to get his car so they could look for Sam.

Payton wrung her hands nervously. "What if we don't find him?"

"We will. Trust me. Please. Sam is like a son to me. I won't lose him," Frank promised.

Neither will I.

Payton pushed some hair back off her face. Composing herself, she looked at Bryce and asked, "Did you see what happened to Sam?"

Bryce shrugged. "I was in front of him. The car hit me, then things went black. I'm sorry, I don't know why Sam isn't nearby."

Payton's eyes grew rounder as she gazed at Frank, then back at Bryce. "You didn't see the guy grab Sam?" Payton continued her questioning. A feeling of hope surged inside her.

Bryce shook his head.

"If he didn't grab him, where the hell is he?" Frank said aloud.

Bryce sniffed the air. Turning around, he faced the direction that the car had left in. "Sam may have shifted." Bryce ran down the street, with Frank and Payton not far behind him.

One of the police officers caught up quickly in the police vehicle. One officer remained at the house just in case anyone returned.

While the officer drove, Payton sat in the front passenger seat while Bryce and Frank sat in the back, watching the streets for any sign of the car or Sam.

After a slight bend in the road, Payton suddenly cried out, "There's the sedan. It's empty."

The grey sedan was parked haphazardly to the side of the road. Brian had obviously run off to hide.

"Do you sense anything?" Frank asked.

"No... Wait... I am picking up a faint feeling of Sam. He's nearby." Payton felt as though she had been struck in the stomach. She tapped frantically at the officer's arm. "Stop the car!"

The car came to an abrupt stop. She jumped out of the police cruiser. "He's hurt." Payton ran in the direction she felt Sam was located.

Bryce kept pace with her as they backtracked on foot about ten feet. In a ditch, a few feet back from the road, they found Sam lying on his side, unconscious. He was naked. "He shifted alright," Bryce noted.

Payton eased herself down the bank, praying that Sam was alive. She knelt beside him as her heart pounded in her chest.

He had a pulse, but it was faint. Payton could feel Frank and Bryce watching in silent worry.

Payton closed her eyes and placed one of her hands on Sam's arm and one on his bare chest, leaning down close to him. "Please come back to me, Sam," she whispered, then held her breath as she waited for her powers to heal him.

It felt like ages before Payton could feel Sam's breathing improve. She opened her eyes and looked down at Sam's face as his eyes flitted open.

"We've gotta stop meeting like this," she grinned in relief.

"It looks like I owe you another one," Sam croaked.

She glanced up at Frank and Bryce. "He's awake."

Looking relieved, Frank announced, "I've called for an ambulance."

"Cancel it. I'm fine," Sam's groggy voice mumbled.

Payton called up to Frank, "Cancel it. He's going to be fine."

Sam gave Payton a weak smile. Payton's eyes were moist. "Oh, my god. I thought I'd lost you," she breathed, tenderly smoothing down Sam's hair. She moved in closer. Brushing his forehead with her lips, Payton thanked the universe that he was alive. She didn't care who saw her affection for Sam and somehow doubted that Frank would be surprised by her actions.

Sam stirred, then moved to sit upright. Payton kept her eyes on his face, blinking back tears as she stood, helping him steady himself so he could stand.

Payton crawled back up to the street, with Sam next to her.

When they both stood in front of Frank and Bryce, Frank asked, "What happened?"

Sam shook his head, not noticing or caring that he was stark naked on the side of the road. He smoothed his hand along his jaw. "I shifted as soon as I saw the guy was driving off. After he hit Bryce, I kept running after him. For some reason, I couldn't maintain my bear form. Each time I got close to the car, I'd shift back to my human form. Finally, he stopped, and I thought he was going to get out of the car. When I reached the driver's side, the window was down, and he had a gun aimed at me... He shot me in the shoulder. I fell backwards, and everything went black. I guess that's how I ended up here." Sam pursed his lips and pointed at the spot Payton had found him. He rubbed his shoulder, then examined it. Payton hadn't seen a bullet wound, and there was no blood on Sam. She wondered if he'd been hit with some sort of tranquillizer gun?

"His car is further up the road, but he's gone." Frank motioned toward the vehicle.

"Damn it," said Sam, scratching his head. "We were so close."

Payton put her hands on her hips. She'd been keeping her eyes fixed on Sam's face because of his state of undress. Now that he was healed and being his regular self, it was far more distracting standing so close to him.

"Can we get to the car, please? Sam needs to get dressed." Payton blushed.

CHAPTER NINE

PAYTON WAS RELIEVED that the police continued to watch the house while Bryce and Sam slept. Payton had insisted that Frank go home for the rest of the night. He gave in, telling them he would see them at work in the morning.

Unable to sleep, Payton sat in her room on her bed, holding an open book in her hands. She was disappointed that Brian was still out there and angry at what he'd done to Sam and Bryce. She hoped that the next time Brian showed himself, she would be ready for him, and no one else would have to be hurt to take him down.

As the sun rose, Payton could hear movement in the house. Someone was awake.

She left her room and went to the kitchen.

Bryce was seated at the table with a cup of coffee in hand. His hair was tousled, and he barely looked up from his cup when she entered the room. He had slept on the couch, and judging from the look of him, Payton gathered he hadn't slept well.

On the other hand, Sam was not only wholly healed and well-rested, but he was also downright cheerful.

"Good morning." He grinned from ear to ear at Payton, then made himself a cup of coffee. "I had a great sleep." He bragged. "Whatever it is your healing power does, you should bottle it and sell it. I feel incredible."

Payton pouted as she tilted her head toward Bryce and grinned. "I healed him too, but he doesn't look as chipper as you do." She was relieved that Sam was okay. She had been terrified at the prospect of him being hurt, or worse. Finding him unconscious had given her a fright, but thankfully he was no worse for wear.

Payton was still a little annoyed that Sam had charged out after Brian, despite her telling him that the man had threatened to kill him.

Bryce looked up and gave a half-smile. "I'm okay. I don't sleep well when I'm not in my own bed. Besides, I think Sam required a bit more healing than I did," he grumbled.

Sam and Payton chuckled.

After breakfast, the trio headed in to work. When Payton and Sam reached their desks, Payton finally turned to Sam, looking perturbed. "I tell you what. If I ever see Brian again, he will pay for everything he's done. I can't believe what he's put us both through."

"I feel the same way. If I could have gotten my hands on him last night, we would be having a very different day today," Sam admitted.

Sam's phone rang, and Payton busied herself on her computer while he took the call. When he hung up, he stood. "Frank wants to see us in his office."

Payton stood, following alongside Sam toward the corridor that led to Frank's office. A few steps into the hallway, Payton's cell phone pinged. She stopped and pulled out her phone. "I've got a text. Hang on." She glanced at the phone and up at Sam, who was eyeing the phone with suspicion.

"It's okay. It's Di. She wants me to pop by as soon as possible," said Payton.

"If you hang on, I'll come with you after we finish with Frank," Sam offered.

Payton waved her hand. "No need. I'll be back in less than an hour. Tell Frank where I went." She nodded toward Sam and headed back out to the elevators.

She hoped everything was okay at Di's shop.

DI'S SHOP WAS DEAD quiet when Payton entered. The bell over the door echoed as she stepped inside. She looked around for Di and quickly located her and the shop mascot, Mr. Baldrick, seated on one of the small sofas on one wall.

Di looked surprised to see her and stood up. "What are you doing here?"

"You sent me a text asking me to get over here right away?" said Payton, with a tilt of her head.

Di shook her head. "Wasn't me? I lost my phone a couple of days ago. I don't know where it is."

Payton's psychic senses tingled. If it wasn't Di, who texted her, who had?

Di put her hands on her hips. "I think it's finally time to close up the shop. I've had virtually no business all week. Things have gotten so bad out there. There aren't many shops left open," Di said, looking lost.

The store was Di's life. Payton knew it would be hard for Di to manage without it. But Payton knew it would be safer if Di stayed at her home and away from the downtown area.

"I have worried about you all along. There are attacks on shopkeepers a few times a week. I don't think there are any normal humans left in town. It's unknown how many supernaturals have turned against us. It's probably for the best if you stay home," Payton said. She glanced at the giant rat seated close by. "What about Mr. Baldrick? What will happen to him?"

Di patted Mr. Baldricks' head. "He's agreed to come home with me. I'll set up a place for him to stay until we can get back to normal here."

Mr. Baldrick waved at Payton. She smiled back. "I'll miss you both." Payton turned her attention back to Di, who was studying her.

"Have you learned anything further about the murders?" Di asked.

Payton smoothed her hair. "We've arrested a Fallen Immortal that knows Lucius, but she isn't saying much. Still, I have a feeling we are closer to stopping him and the problems he caused." Payton pushed her shoulders back and smiled at Di.

"Right. Well, let's hope things improve soon. The town out there now is not the Sylvan Falls I know and love," said Di, grimacing.

Payton smiled and hugged Di. "I better get back to work. I said I'd only be gone a short time. Call me if you need anything. I hope you find your phone," said Payton, wondering who could have taken Di's phone and why?

She left the shop and headed toward her car a couple of doors down from Di's shop.

PAYTON OPENED HER DRIVER'S side door and flinched when something sharp struck her right arm. She looked down to see a dart that had pierced through her clothing.

Its effects were immediate, causing her to feel drowsy.

She pulled out the offending object and quickly scanned the area. Hurried footsteps echoed along the sidewalk from her left while two men rushed at her from the right.

A wave of dizziness struck while her legs wobbled beneath her. Forcing her legs to move, she attempted to push her body into the driver's seat. Failing miserably, her legs dangled outside while her body was only halfway on the car seat.

Suddenly, the men were at her side.

"What are you doing?" She jerked her arm from the grasp of one man. When they continued to reach for her, she attempted to cast magic at them. Her head was spinning. Growing weaker with each movement, it was becoming harder to keep her eyes open.

She felt powerful arms pull her away from the driver's side, then hold her upright. Brian Thomas stepped up with something in his hands.

He barked, "take her."

"Where are you taking me?"

Two men held her firmly by her arms as she used her remaining strength to struggle against them.

Finally, a sack was placed over her head, and she felt herself being lifted off the ground. She opened her mouth to object as everything went black.

CHAPTER TEN

THE SMELL OF DUST AND stale air filled Payton's nostrils as she roused her eyes, still closed. Her head ached as she tried to recall where she was.

Her eyes flew open. *No!*

A dim light shone through the fabric of the bag that had been draped over her head. The memory of what happened came flooding back, filling her with dread. She remembered Brian's face as one of her abductors.

Trying to remain as calm as possible, she listened to her captors speaking in hushed tones. It wasn't clear how many people were in the room with her or where she was being held.

She hoped Sam would realize by now that she was missing and start searching for her. Tears threatened as a ragged sigh escaped her lips. *Poor Sam*. He would blame himself, even though it wasn't his fault she was taken. She bemoaned her situation. Wishing she had let him go with her to Di's.

Payton tried not to make any sudden moves, hoping her captors would think she was still knocked out, giving her time to develop a plan. She reached out with her psychic senses, only to find she didn't have any. *What the hell?*

Not only was Payton unable to feel anything on a psychic level. She also couldn't use her telepathy or magic.

Perspiration covered her face. Panic set in, making it hard to breathe normally.

Crap! What have they done to me? She lifted her head upright, wondering how many people Brian had involved in his insidious plot to abduct her.

"Looks like she's waking up," said a male voice.

She was seated upright and soon realized she couldn't move her hands, finding they were restrained together in her lap. Her legs were tied to the chair in which she sat.

Heavy footsteps approached, and the sack was pulled from Payton's head. She blinked as her eyes adjusted to the light in the room. Glancing around, she noticed two single-paned curtainless windows to her right. It was still daylight. She obviously hadn't been asleep for very long.

The smell of sawdust and dirt filled the air. A quick assessment of her situation told Payton she was in what appeared to be a barn.

The walls were made of faded wood panels. The floor was dirt and sawdust. The only light aside from the windows was a bare lightbulb hanging in the centre of the room. An orange extension cord ran from it across the ceiling and out through a hole in the wall. Scattered around the interior were several wooden chairs.

One wall had a tattered sofa up against it, with a small wooden table in front of it. Remnants of food and drink were littered here and there. From the angle she had been placed, she could not see a way out of the barn.

All eyes were on her as she took in her surroundings. On the sofa, staring back at her with curiosity was a woman with cropped purple hair. Next to her were two men. Each was well built in a sleek, muscular kind of way.

I'll bet they're Shifters, thought Payton.

On the far wall, two tall men stood watching her. Judging from their height, she would bet money that they were Fallen Ones.

Payton's body tensed at seeing the people standing closest to her. Just feet away, Brian was sitting in a chair, leering at her. Next to him was a tall woman with angry azure coloured eyes.

"Go get Lucius," she commanded someone behind Payton.

Payton's eyes were saucers. *Lucius? Shit!*

This was not how she had intended to meet her enemy. She felt queasy at the thought.

"What have you done to me?" she barked aloud.

No one spoke. Payton didn't have to wait long before the roguish, well-dressed, six-foot-something man with slick, dark brown hair and piercing brown eyes sauntered around her from behind.

Standing before Payton was the man from her nightmares. The man who mercilessly killed her grandfather, Basil. The monster who had gone out with and probably killed her neighbour, Mandy. She struggled with her restraints, trying to free herself.

"Hello, Payton. It is good to see you again," Lucius said in a smooth voice.

"I can't say the same." She cut her eyes at Lucius while wrestling to free her hands from the restraints.

With a smug look, he pointed toward the bonds that held her. "There is no point in trying to escape. You can't."

Feeling weakened and angry about being unable to use any of her abilities, Payton screwed up her face. "Tell me what you've done to me?" she roared.

He took a step forward, a sly smile on his lips. "Ah yes, Brian here can nullify all supernatural powers. You are... essentially helpless."

Payton felt fury, but it wasn't building to the fever pitch it usually did. Where was the ancient power inside asking to be released?

Instantly, it all made sense. Each time Payton had been around Brian, she had felt her energy change, becoming weaker. It also explained what happened to Sam when he tried to shift and failed to do so.

So much for fighting her way out. She was tight-lipped as she squinted at Lucius.

Lucius thrust his chin in the air. “Fortunately, Immortals not born of this planet are immune to his ability.”

Payton closed her eyes for a moment and tried to call out to Frank in her mind. She popped them back open when she realized she would not hear him if he responded.

Lucius waggled his finger in front of her. “Tsk Tsk... Such a stubborn thing. If you are doing what I think you are, no one is coming to rescue you. Only Immortal Guardians can sense you, and... oops... there aren’t any in Sylvan Falls.” He put his fingers over his lips in a mocking gesture.

The realization that Lucius wasn’t aware of Joshua flashed through her mind. She quickly replaced the thought and put a block up to keep out any other telepaths that might be in the room. She knew that Fallen Immortals lost their telepathic ability in their downfall. Though it appeared that they knew how to block their thoughts if Nadia was any indication.

Payton cast an eye around the room once again and remarked, “That’s a lot of thugs to hold one woman. What are you afraid of, Lucius?”

Lucius stepped closer to Payton. Grabbing a nearby chair, he placed it a couple of feet in front of her and sat down to face her.

She studied him. “I suppose it was you who sent the threatening notes?”

“Not exactly. I sent Brian out to watch you and report back to me. I never expected him to become obsessed with you... He took liberties, I’ll admit. But one look at you again, and I can see why he would want you all to himself. You are quite striking. Even more so than your mother was.”

“You leave my mother out of this,” Payton spat.

“You are far more tenacious than your mother was,” he said wryly.

Payton narrowed her eyes. "Why were you watching me?" She prayed Lucius's cocky, self-assured nature would make it easy to get information from him.

"I wanted to know more about you before bringing you to me. Fortunately for me, I was able to put my people in place at The Agency to help me with my mission."

"What are you talking about? Why?" Payton asked with disgust.

Lucius leaned forward with his hands on his thighs. "You have no idea who you are, do you?"

"Tell me why I'm here and stop playing around," Payton snarked.

Lucius eyed her with a lustful gaze. He licked his lips. "I haven't even begun to play around. There's so much to discuss first."

Payton sneered at him. "I don't know what you hope to accomplish by abducting me. I won't help you."

With a devious smile, he said, "What I *hope* to do is illuminate the truth for you. I gather you are unaware of what you are? With my help, you will begin to understand Immortality and what it means for you moving forward."

Payton was mystified. Did he not know that Azrael had trained her? She hadn't realized that Joshua and Azrael had done such an excellent job hiding from Lucius's contacts within The Agency. That was something, at least.

"What makes you think I'm an Immortal?"

He threw his head back in an exaggerated laugh. "I am not a fool." Leaning closer with his lips curled, he whispered, "Who do you think ran you off the road?" Sitting back, looking pleased with himself, he put a hand to his chest. "Imagine my surprise when you came back from the dead?"

Payton gave him a death stare and struggled against her restraints once more. "I knew it was you. You sick bastard! When I get free from here, you will pay for what you've done," she hollered.

He scoffed. "You won't be going anywhere, my dear woman. There are three other Fallen Immortals in this room aside from myself. Even if you could free yourself from your restraints. You could never take on all four of us and the supernatural humans that surround you."

Payton's eyes shot daggers at Lucius. "We'll see about that." She was unafraid and sought only to end the terror that this mad man insisted on inflicting on the town.

Lucius played with his chin as he watched Payton's anger grow. The corners of his mouth curled as he cast his eyes over her.

"You killed Mandy, didn't you?" she asked, changing the subject.

He flicked his hand as if he was swatting away a fly. "Humph.... annoying human. I only needed her to get near you. She wasn't much use to me after that."

Payton felt sick at the thought of her poor neighbour dying only because she lived next to her. Maybe Nadia was right. It looked as though Lucius would stop at nothing to get her in his grasp. Payton's jaw clenched as she glared at Lucius.

Her thoughts were interrupted by the sound of Brian breathing loudly next to her. Payton turned her face in his direction to see him gawking at her and licking his lips. The creep made her skin crawl. "Piss off, jerk."

Brian's eyes flashed with anger, but he didn't make a move toward her.

Returning her eyes to Lucius, with disgust evident on her face, she tilted her head in Brian's direction. "Does he have to be here?"

Lucius raised a brow. "Until I know you will behave, he will remain nearby."

Brian stood, taking a step toward Payton. "You promised me, master. You said she would be mine," Brian whined.

Lucius gave Brian a warning look.

Payton looked down at the floor, irritated with Brian's pervy energy. She felt sick at the idea that she might be handed off to Brian when Lucius was finished with her. There was no way she was going to allow that to happen.

Wishing she could free herself from the restraints, she focused on keeping Lucius talking. She had to buy herself as much time as possible to give Sam and her father a chance to find her.

Lucius's voice became soft, his expression unreadable as he turned his attention back to Payton. "We are a lot alike, you and me. We both have been cast out by our own kind. You from the witch community and me from the Immortal Guardians."

Payton's lip curled. "We are nothing alike. You kill people and have others kill for you. Don't compare me to you."

"Don't act so innocent. I have had my people watching you for a while. I know you have killed as well... How did it feel the first time you unleashed your true Immortal power?" He raised one brow.

Payton gave him a dark look. Remaining silent.

"What? Nothing to say? That's not like you, Miss Adams," he smirked.

She had to know how he knew so much about her. "When did you discover who I was?" she asked, already sensing Lucius had known all along.

"Not long after you moved to Sylvan Falls. After I met you that day outside your house, I knew for certain. I assume you are the result of Rebekah Chartwell's affair with the tiresome Immortal Guardian, Joshua?"

Payton pressed her lips, narrowing her eyes at him.

"Your mother chose an Immortal Guardian over me. The foolish woman...." His eyes changed. "Your mother was a powerful witch with an even more powerful father. She could have ruled this town. But she turned her back on all of it. Pity." He looked past Payton as if remembering something.

At that moment, Payton felt a sense of pride. She was grateful her mother dared to leave Sylvan Falls. It had been the right thing to do.

"My mother didn't want to be part of the witch community. She wanted a normal life. There is nothing wrong with that. And why would she want a Fallen One like you? She feared you. Is it any wonder she didn't want you?" Payton mocked.

Disappointment flickered in his eyes. "Rebekah's loss." He stood and approached Payton, putting out one hand and stroking her cheek. "Now I have you. You are twice as powerful as your mother ever was."

Payton recoiled, closing her eyes.

Lucius dropped his hands to his side and continued to stand in front of her. "Together, we will take back Sylvan Falls and make it as it should have been. People will follow us when they see our true power combined."

"Over my dead body... I don't want to control anyone. Least of all, with you at my side," Payton spat.

Lucius shoved his shoulders back and looked down at her. "I'm going to tell you a little secret." He lowered his voice, "your grandparents were not the first Chartwells I have taken the life of. I have been following your family's line for centuries. Frequently, I have been able to make the Chartwell warlocks do my bidding. You will be no exception. You will join me as your ancestors have."

Payton scoffed. "There is no way in hell I am doing your bidding. What are you going to do? Kill me like you killed my grandparents?" she thrust her neck forward, daring him to do something.

Lucius frowned. "Don't you see? Because of the Chartwell connection, it is destiny that you join me." He tilted his head. "That... or I will make you suffer for eternity. One of the great things about all Immortals is that they can be tortured for centuries. They die and regenerate hundreds of times just to go through it all again. Imagine being buried alive in a coffin, then running out of air, dying, and waking to the same prison over and over for thousands of years."

Payton shuddered. She would rather die than endure torture.

"I may not have a way to find Immortal Guardians right now, but I soon will. When I do, none of you will be safe. Even if it takes a hundred years, you *will* join me. You will come around to my way of thinking, and I will have your loyalty."

CHAPTER ELEVEN

SAM HUNG UP HIS PHONE, letting out a long, exasperated sigh. His meeting with Frank had ended over an hour earlier. Now he sat watching the clock and thrumming his fingers on his desk. "Where are you, Payton?" He sighed.

Mark and Alex entered the office, smiling as they chatted to one another.

Mark stopped. The smile slid from his lips as he walked over to Sam's desk. "What's wrong? Where's Payton?" he asked, glancing at her empty chair.

Sam stood, putting his hands out to the side. "That's what I'd like to know. She left a couple of hours ago. She should have been back by now."

"Where did she say she was going?" asked Alex.

"To see her friend... I've called the friend, but she said Payton left almost an hour and a half ago." Sam shook his head.

"Let's go see if we can find her," said Mark, heading back out of the office with Sam and Alex close behind.

"I should have gone with her," Sam agonized.

"Don't worry. We'll find Payton," said Mark, glancing at Sam.

When they reached operations, Sam paused. "I'm going to tell Frank what's happening. Wait here," he said, striding off.

Frank looked up from his desk as Sam stood with his hands holding each side of the door frame. "Something has happened to Payton. Alex, Mark and I are going to look for her."

Frank jumped up and walked around his desk. "I'm coming with you. Fill me in on the way."

ALEX DROVE THE GROUP to Main Street, where they saw Payton's vehicle parked near Di's shop. He pulled in behind Payton's car, and the men jumped out to look around.

"It looks like she was getting into her car when she was taken. Her keys are on the floor on the driver's side," said Frank. He reached in and picked up the keys. Worry etched his face.

Sam ran a hand through his hair and growled loudly. Glancing down on the sidewalk next to the driver's side of the vehicle, he picked up a small dart. "Brian!" He spat, kneading his shoulder with the memory of the night before. "I think the same type of dart was used on me last night."

Frank took the dart into his own hand and examined it. "This doesn't look good. It means they would have knocked her out. She could be anywhere." He put the dart in his pocket, his jaw set.

Sam felt fury at the idea of Brian touching Payton. He needed to find her!

"Do you have any idea where she might have been taken?" asked Alex.

Sam paced back and forth for a moment with clenched fists. He stopped and looked at the other three men. "Maybe... Payton and I found out that Lucius is in a farmhouse at the edge of town. Payton had a feeling that Brian and Lucius might be working together. If he is involved in her abduction, they likely took her there." It didn't make

Sam feel much better knowing that it wasn't only Brian that was with Payton, but the same Immortal that had killed her family.

Frank nodded toward Payton's vehicle. "In either case, I think we need Joshua. He will be able to feel her presence if we get close enough to her. I'll take her vehicle back to HQ and get Joshua." He spoke directly to Sam. "You three head to the area you mentioned. Call me with the location once you are there," Frank stated before climbing into the vehicle and taking off.

Sam had Alex drive while he and Mark observed the streets and farms for any sign of activity that could lead them to Payton. Dread twisted in his gut. He knew Payton could not be permanently killed, but she could certainly be harmed, or worse. The thought of someone putting their hands on her filled him with rage. *I should have gone with her.* He hoped Joshua could locate her quickly.

Meanwhile, he would do everything in his power to find her on his own. If Brian was responsible for her abduction, Sam would make sure he paid for harming her.

He surveyed the farmland outside, praying that he would have the chance to see Payton's beautiful face again.

After driving back and forth several times, the men narrowed the search area down to a two-mile radius and waited for Frank and Joshua.

He did not know Lucius's plan for Payton but hoped it didn't involve taking her away from Sylvan Falls. Sam ground his jaw, thinking about everything they had already been through in the months they had known one another.

He couldn't imagine her not being at his side. She meant so much to him, and he had a feeling she cared about him just as much, though she seemed reluctant to admit it.

"I hope Joshua and Frank get here soon. Every minute that we lose, they could be harming Payton." Sam scowled.

CHAPTER TWELVE

PAYTON SHOVED HER HEAD forward, lifting her chin. "You are a psychopath... You will never have my loyalty!"

Lucius smoothed her long brown hair with one hand as she twisted her head from his grasp, giving him a dirty look.

"If you do not join me and the Immortal Guardians become aware of your existence, they will see you as a threat. Believe me when I tell you... You do not want that."

"What makes you say that? Who's saying that other Fallen Immortals don't already see me as a threat? Since you seem to have told everyone that you know about me?"

"Those that follow me understand you are meant to be on our side. You, too, will come to see that in time. I assure you, the Guardians will not want you to exist. They will fear you. Even if they don't try to lock you away, they will still want to use you as a weapon."

Payton huffed out some air, surveying Lucius. "What? And you won't, I suppose?"

Lucius pressed his lips, looking disappointed. Payton awaited a response, but the Fallen One changed the subject. "I'm sure you're wondering why I am going to so much trouble," Lucius began.

Payton shook her head. "Not really."

Ignoring her comment, Lucius continued speaking. "You see, it's too late for Sylvan Falls. The town is basically mine already. Right now, my followers are taking back the town right under the noses of those who wish to subjugate them.... Everything is in place, allowing me to rule over the town that should have always been mine," he said, oozing with overconfidence.

Payton was skeptical of his explanation. "Is that it?... Is that what this is all about?"

The Fallen One gave a derisive snort. "This? Oh no. This is just the beginning. We have been setting things up around the world for centuries. I carefully placed Fallen Immortals and humans in positions of power... Some wars had to be waged to create the fear required... The planet itself had to be brought to the brink of death, but we can pull it back if enough humans are removed."

"Everything that has occurred has been done to ensure my plan came together. Now it is finally time... The planet is ripe for domination. I have been waiting for this moment... When I could take my place as the ruler of this world. The only thing left is to get rid of all those who do not stand with me. And of course, to have you at my side."

Payton laughed. Is this what happens when you are an evil mastermind that lives forever? *He's not just a psychopath... he's bloody delusional.*

Lucius glared at her. His mouth was down-turned.

"I still don't see how *I* fit into your plan for world domination," she retorted.

Lucius leaned forward. "All will be revealed in good time. Your presence is a bonus. Once I have taken Sylvan Falls, I will increase the size of my army of supernatural beings. They will spread out and do their job bringing the human population under control."

Payton shook her head. "If your ultimate plan is to kill humans, then why kill supernaturals here in Sylvan Falls?"

"Some supernatural beings have the foolish idea they should protect humans. Taking care of those creatures first allows us to do whatever we want to humans. It also has the desired effect of pushing more humans out of Sylvan Falls... It's a win, win." Lucius put his palms up toward the ceiling as he explained.

Payton grunted. "I can't see you getting supernaturals to agree to kill humans. You will fail in your mission. Besides, humans have every right to be here alongside us."

Lucius's face contorted with anger. "Humans don't deserve this jewel of a planet; they have sought only to destroy it! I don't have to be an Immortal Guardian to know that if the population is reduced, the Earth will thrive again."

Payton was growing tired of speaking to the jerk. She wanted to get out of the barn so she could warn Frank and the others about the Fallen Immortal's dark plan. "So noble of you," Payton said with sarcasm. "You say you want to save the planet, but what you really want is to be worshipped and obeyed."

Stepping back, Lucius took her in while a fake smile plastered his face. Payton didn't need her psychic powers to know he was a manipulative asshat.

Looking determined, he stretched out one hand. "I see the value in you, Payton. The value of us as a team. I know what your magical ancestors were capable of. The power you possess as an immortal and a witch...is unfathomable. Allow me to train you."

Leaning her head forward, she looked Lucius in the eye as she sneered.

"Never!"

CHAPTER THIRTEEN

ERWIN, A WARLOCK WITH shoulder-length brown hair, hurried to the Elder Council chambers. His heart raced with nervous energy. He was about to interrupt several of the town's most powerful witches and warlocks. His role as an assistant to one of the Elders was usually a dry, tedious job. Today, it looked as though everything could be about to change.

Standing upright and out of breath from running to the building from downtown, he knocked on the chamber door.

"Come," a male voice called out.

Erwin stepped inside the room, his face pale with worry. "Elders, I am sorry for the interruption, but there is an uprising in town. Supernatural beings are fighting in the streets and destroying anything in their wake."

The men and women shared worried glances before one warlock responded.

"Why should we concern ourselves with the violence? Haven't enough of our kind died at the hands of this darkness?"

One witch spoke, putting her hand up. "Have you seen this firsthand?" she asked the young warlock.

Erwin nodded, wiping sweat from his brow. "Yes... and the violence appears to be spreading."

The powerful senior warlock, a bronze-skinned man named Therrien, waved his hand to create a magic *seeing* circle directly in front of him. The energy swirled briefly before showing an image of downtown Sylvan Falls. He could see hundreds of people trashing the shops and fighting with one another in the street. Therrien's chocolate-coloured eyes widened with alarm at the sight. "It would seem things have taken an even darker turn," he said, shutting down the seeing circle and gazing at the table of Elders.

"We need to stop this, or there will be no town left," said a female on the opposite side of the round table.

Everyone present nodded in agreement.

"I will contact the Supreme Elder. We must gather as many from the witch community as possible," said Therrien.

Erwin stood at attention with his arms tight to his side. "What can I do to help?"

Therrien stood and looked at Erwin. "Gather as many members of the magic community as possible." He moved his eyes to the group now standing around the table. "Start with contacting anyone that you know personally and ask them to spread the word. We will meet outside Chartwell Academy in an hour."

The Elders exchanged worried glances before hurrying out of the room.

THERRIEN NEVER CARED much for Margret. And not just because she was chosen over him as Supreme Elder when Basil Chartwell died. But because she saw everyone outside the magic community as the enemy. Her unfairness over the years towards some young witch and warlock students had also drawn his attention time and again, forcing him to intervene.

They rarely saw eye to eye, and he wasn't sure what she had gotten herself into of late. She had not shown her face at the office in some time. Therrien was the only Elder who knew Margret, the Supreme Elder, was hiding, though he didn't know her exact location.

He pulled out his phone and called her.

"What is it, Therrien?" Margret's voice had its usual curt tone.

"The town appears to be going to hell. I have just become aware of fighting, looting and general chaos downtown. I'm gathering as many from our community as are willing to stop this."

Therrien knew that if he didn't tell her about his plan, there would be hell to pay when she found out. She had a way of making everyone's life more difficult if she didn't get her way.

"Send someone to pick me up immediately."

Therrien was taken aback. "Are you sure?"

"Yes. I know more about what's happening than any of you," Margret stated before giving him her location.

"Perhaps you wouldn't mind sharing some of what you know? What are we dealing with out there?" Therrien asked.

Margret paused a moment. "Fallen Immortals. One, in particular, is extremely dangerous. They are invulnerable to magic, but we can stop everyone else if there are enough of us," Margret's voice wavered. "Apparently, there are two types of Immortals. Guardians and Fallen Ones. Until recently, I did not know that was the case."

Exasperated, Therrien blasted her. "Are you telling me there have been Fallen Immortals under our nose this entire time, and you didn't advise the council?"

"I told you I was not aware of them. I assure you!"

Therrien was shaking his head and frowning. "You have been going on about Immortal threats for decades. You swore up and down that they run The Paranormal and Supernatural Agency. What type of Immortal is running The Agency, if any?"

"Guardians.... I think," Margret responded.

"What else have you not told the council?" Therrien asked.

"Nothing.... Really. I... there is one Guardian that I have recently become aware of. She is Basil Chartwell's granddaughter."

"Rebekah has a daughter?" he was shocked. Rebekah had left town and was never heard from again. He had always wondered what had happened to her.

"Yes. But the child has no interest in being part of the magic community."

Therrien scowled. *Unbelievable.* "Tsk... We have much to discuss when this is over, Margret. The council will not be pleased when they learn you withheld such important information.... Supreme Elder or not, you can be voted out for such a thing!" Therrien threatened.

"We are wasting time arguing about this now. Are you going to send someone to get me or not?" Margaret's voice was shrill.

"I'm on my way to you now!" Therrien pulled his keys from his pocket and hurried out of the building. He couldn't believe what Margret had told him. He wondered if some of her insane rules were connected to the knowledge of Basil Chartwell's grandchild and not just her idea that Immortals were dangerous.

CHAPTER FOURTEEN

BACK AT THE AGENCY Headquarters, Joshua was sitting in quiet meditation when a frantic knock on his door brought him back to the room. He stood, sensing it was Frank and not Payton at his door since there was no Immortal presence.

Upon opening the door, he saw a pale and panic-stricken Frank. His heart sank at the realization that something must have happened to his daughter. There would be no other reason for Frank to be knocking on his door.

"What has happened to Payton?"

Frank rubbed his cheek. "She's been taken. We need your help to locate her."

Joshua tensed. "How long has she been missing?"

"She left a couple of hours ago and hasn't returned. Sam and a couple of Agents are waiting for us," Frank breathed.

Joshua wondered if Lucius had taken her or if it was the stalker she had told him about. He hoped the latter since Lucius had a way to hide his Immortal essence. Which might mean he could also hide Payton's.

"Let's go." He made a move to leave.

Frank hesitated. "Do you want to disguise yourself? What if we run into staff on the way up in the elevator? They may recognize you?"

Joshua didn't care. His daughter needed him, and he was the only one who could locate her. Though he would need to be within a mile of Payton to sense her strongly. "I do not think that matters now. We must find Payton as soon as possible. If Lucius is behind this, he will try to manipulate her. He will want her to join him and will stop at nothing to achieve his goal." Joshua scowled.

He had not felt such intense emotions since he left Rebekah to go to Europe. His one true love had insisted on remaining behind in the small town of Harper's Creek. The guilt and sadness over the loss of Rebekah had followed him wherever he went. He never embarked on another love relationship after Rebekah. He could not. Instead, he had hidden away in a monastery, pondering his Immortal existence without her. Finding out he and Rebekah had a daughter gave him purpose once more.

Learning that Payton was born Immortal, as well as a powerful witch, was a blessing *and* a curse. On the one hand, they would have eternity to get to know one another. On the other hand, the sword spoken of in the prophecy could bring about her downfall. That was if Lucius didn't manage to turn her first. The thought of losing his only child scared him more than he cared to acknowledge aloud.

He wished Payton did not have to use the sword but feared it was the only way to bring peace to Sylvan Falls once again.

Frank led the way to the elevator, and the men stepped inside. "I've got a car waiting outside. Sam has texted his location, and we'll meet him there. Apparently, he and Payton had scouted the area earlier after being told Lucius was hiding on one of the farm properties. It's all we have to go on right now."

Joshua half-listened to Frank as the elevator doors closed, and moments later, opened at street level. With his head down and his thoughts elsewhere, he marched past the tall, ginger-haired security guard standing at the entrance to the elevator without noticing him.

Neither he nor Frank noticed the recognition on the guard's face or his angry glare as they left the Sylvan Falls Museum.

CHAPTER FIFTEEN

LUCIUS REACHED INTO his pocket to take out his ringing phone. Not taking his eyes off Payton, he answered. "This better be good. I asked not to be disturbed."

Payton couldn't hear what the voice was saying on the other end of the phone, but judging from the look of surprise on the Fallen One's face, it wasn't good news.

"When did they leave?" Lucius asked the caller. He glared at Payton as he spoke. "Fine. Go ahead. Do it now," he said, finishing the call and putting the phone in his pocket.

He narrowed his eyes at Payton. "That was Rufus. A Fallen Immortal who was recently hired as a security guard at The Agency. He just informed me he recognized a former adversary...." Lucius's nostrils flared. "Rufus assured me that the man he just saw leaving The Agency was none other than Joshua Adams."

Lucius closed the distance between him and Payton. He placed his hands down hard on top of hers as he leaned in. "When were you going to tell me about your father being back in Sylvan Falls?"

Payton's brows rose. Lucius's eyes were black with rage. She could see he was pissed, but she wasn't afraid. "It looks like you're running out of time to make me see your point of view. Isn't that right, master?" she mocked.

The Fallen Immortal's face was red with rage. He raised one open hand and smacked Payton hard across the face. Her head jerked to one side as the slap resounded throughout the barn.

The sting in Payton's cheek only fed her growing hatred for Lucius. She straightened. Her lip curled. "When I get out of here, I am going to kill you," she crowed.

In a fit of frenzy, Lucius punched her this time.

She tasted blood as her lip split. Brian ran forward with his hands up in the air. "Master, don't damage her face," he fretted.

Lucius ignored him and glared at Payton. "Join me!" he insisted as he hit her again and again.

Her head bounced back and forth with the force of each blow. Her cheeks throbbed, and she could feel the skin around her eyes swelling. Refusing to show fear or give him what he wanted, she laughed at him through painful lips.

"Is that all you've got?" she jeered, holding back tears from the pain he was inflicting.

He stared at her, incredulous. "If you know what's good for you...you will join me."

Payton glared at Lucius in silent protest as a single tear ran down her cheek.

"Then you will suffer," he threatened, punching her a few more times.

Eyeing her enemy through swollen eyes, Payton spat out blood. Through split lips and a bloodied nose, she forced her mouth to form the word.

"Never!"

Lucius began another ruthless attack, striking her in the stomach this time. Payton coughed as her upper body thrust forward in agony. Her face and head thumped. Her ribs ached. Her stomach spasmed with each punch.

Payton wasn't sure how long she could endure the thrashing, and she regretted taunting him the way she had. *Hurry.* Payton prayed her father and Sam would find her soon. Her bravado was threatening to slip. She didn't want Lucius to see any weakness in her.

She could see that Lucius was panic-stricken at the thought of her father coming to find her. There was no way of knowing what Lucius would do now that he knew she wasn't the only Immortal Guardian in Sylvan Falls.

"Get the van ready. We're leaving," Lucius ground out to those around him. He looked at Payton. "You will be joining us," he bellowed, grabbing Payton's throat with one large hand, cutting off her air supply.

"Master! You're damaging her. Stop!" Brian pleaded, rushing toward Lucius, who, in a blind rage, thrust one arm out to push Brian aside using a little too much force.

Brian lost his balance, falling backward. A horrid thud resounded as his skull cracked on a sharp piece of wood that jutted out from a window ledge. Blood smeared down the wall as he slid to the ground.

Payton immediately sensed he was dead as thoughts flooded her mind from those around her.

Lucius removed his hand from her throat, momentarily distracted by the accidental death of Brian. He gawked awkwardly at the body as it bled out, a look of dismay on his face.

Payton choked and sputtered, taking in large gulps of air. With Payton's abilities fully restored, her eternal power roared to be released. She felt the potent energy swirling through her entire body, filling her with rage, adrenaline, and fortitude.

Payton used her returned strength to break her hands and feet free from the restraints. Checking her pocket for the enchanted medallion, she tossed it aside so her father could find her without anything blocking her energy.

Clenching her fists tight, she stood and felt her body vibrating. She moved her arms away from her sides just a little. The walls of the barn shuddered in response. Furniture began to shift, and the windowpanes rattled. She had never wanted to succumb to her Immortal mana more than she did at that moment.

Lucius stalked back over, stopping short when he realized Payton was affecting the surrounding space. His lips drew back.

In one long stride, she stood less than a foot from Lucius. "I'm not going anywhere with you." She pulled back a fist and brought it forward, striking him hard in the face. His head shot back as he stumbled.

A man's voice echoed from behind them. "Sir, someone's just turned down the driveway!"

Dumbstruck, Lucius wiped at his bloodied nose, pressing his lips together, frowning. He spun on his heel and looked at the other Fallen Immortals, who were hovering nearby in a state of shock. "We have to get a move on." Motioning to the remaining minions, he pointed at Payton. "Take care of this."

He and the other Immortals darted toward an exit at the other end of the building. "Coward!" she shouted, storming after him. "Are you so afraid of me you won't stay and fight?"

Lucius looked over his shoulder at Payton, surrounded by the other Immortals.

"This isn't over. We will meet again. I assure you of that!"

Payton lost sight of Lucius, and the other Fallen Immortals as a large group of supernaturals stormed the barn through the same side door.

They lined up, readying themselves to take their turn against her. She could feel the slow healing of her body taking place, but it did nothing to curb the blind rage that tore through her. Her body pulsated as a feeling of invulnerability flowed within her.

One of the supernaturals cast a flaming fireball in her direction. She diffused it with a water spell. She didn't sense that the man knew magic. His only superpower was likely pyrokinesis.

She glowered at the superhuman. "Are you sure you want to do this?"

He hurled fire at her again in response. This time she threw her hand's palm out, using a magic shield that immediately negated the fire. The onslaught continued as she took turns dodging the fire and putting it out with magic.

Her temper showed no signs of easing off. "You really should stop!" she warned.

The Human-Pyro's attack didn't let up, even though he wasn't getting anywhere with his blasts. Growing tired of the barrage of flames, Payton's expression darkened. It was clear he didn't want to listen to her warnings.

Raising her brows, she muttered, "Suit yourself."

Striding toward the fire thrower with both hands out to the side, electromagnetic energy balls crackled in Payton's palms. He appeared to take no notice of the threat. Payton let out a grunt as she thrust the balls of energy toward him. He fell to the floor in a smoking dead heap.

The rest of the supernatural beings quickly surrounded her.

Payton tilted her head, taking in the crowd. *I can see you all have a death wish.*

At that moment, Payton's fury outranked her common sense. Her body was thrumming with power to the point where she knew it was tipping over the edge. She was thinking of nothing other than wreaking vengeance. It was her turn to fight back, and she was going to make them all pay for what Lucius and Brian put her through.

Knowing she could use magic to stop the confrontation in its tracks, she forwent that in favour of hand-to-hand fighting. She had trained for such an occasion. What she hadn't counted on was her strength escalating with each well-placed blow.

She turned, then lunged at two supernaturals, striking them hard with her fists. Soon she was taking on two at a time while others waited their turn to face her. Or so it seemed to Payton.

Fighting her way through the horde, she flinched when a swift kick contacted her ribcage. One of the shifters had launched himself at her from the left side of the room. "Great," she muttered, whirling to face the man. A swift sidekick sent the male shifter flying.

The female shifter attempted to land a punch, only to have Payton block it with her arm. Payton then thrust her palm hard against the woman's chest, sending her gliding across the room and smashing into the wall. The shifter landed on the floor, unconscious.

One by one, she did battle with those who dared to stand before her. Sounds of shouting drifted in from outside, but she didn't have time or the inclination to tune in psychically to find out what was going on. If they were coming for her, she would take care of them, too.

Payton's body continued to heal as she fought tirelessly. Dried blood pinched the skin on her face. Her senses were heightened to feel her attackers before they got close enough to land a swipe. Each time her fury ebbed, the memories of the assault from Lucius made her blood boil.

After dispensing with most of Lucius's army of supernaturals, she turned to several rather large males that remained standing. She could feel their reservations about fighting her after having watched her take out a dozen or so people.

"What's the matter, boys? Scared of one little lady?" she taunted.

The men looked at one another, then rushed Payton. She launched herself at the one in the middle, wrapping her legs around his waist and pummeling his head until he was too bloodied to see.

When she finished with him, she pushed herself off him. Standing, she put a hand on his arm, gripping it. Using him to balance herself, she thrust a roundhouse kick at another of the men, knocking him out.

The third male fell to his knees, waving his hands in front of him. He cowered at her feet. "I don't wanna fight," he pleaded.

CHAPTER SIXTEEN

DURING THE DRIVE, SAM explained to his shocked colleagues that Payton and Joshua were Immortal Guardians. The night before, he told Bryce the news after Payton healed him. He didn't see any reason not to tell them with everything they were doing to help her.

"So let me get this right," said Alex, looking confused. "This guy... Lucius? He's an Immortal too, but not the same as Payton?"

Sam and his colleagues stood on the side of the road watching for Frank and Joshua. Sam rubbed his brow, wishing they would hurry.

Sam sighed. "Yeah. The way Payton tells it, he was a Guardian but turned against them and became a Fallen One."

Alex rubbed the side of his head. "It sounds crazy. I never imagined there was such a thing."

Sam thought about mentioning Azrael but changed his mind. They would find out about everything when, or if, the time came. For now, they needed to find the only woman he truly cared about opening himself up to.

Mark, seeing he was tense, put a hand on his upper back. "Relax, we'll find her."

Sam pressed his lips. "I'll relax *when* we find her," he grumbled.

Another ten minutes passed as the men stood watching the road in silence. Finally, Sam saw Frank and Joshua approaching in Payton's vehicle. "There they are."

Frank pulled up alongside them. Sam noted the grave expression on Joshua's face. He knew Joshua would also be devastated if anything happened to Payton. He pushed down the lump that rose in his throat.

Frank rolled down the passenger side window to speak to the men on the side of the road. Leaning down to peer out, he asked, "have you checked any of the houses yet?"

Mark answered. "No. We've taken a quick drive around, but nothing seems out of the ordinary, so we haven't ventured down any driveways so far."

Joshua pointed ahead of them. "Let's head in that direction. I will try to sense Payton."

They all agreed, and the three men stepped back from the car. Frank turned the vehicle around and maneuvered to be in front of Alex's SUV. Sam took the passenger's seat while Mark hopped in the back. Alex began to follow Frank.

Sam watched Joshua. The man's head was down as though he were concentrating.

They didn't drive far before Joshua's head suddenly shot back, and he looked out his side window. Frank slowed down.

On his right, he noticed a farm property with a barn and several vehicles parked out front.

"I think he's found her," Alex announced.

Sam bit his lip. *I hope so.*

Joshua pointed out the window in the farm's direction.

Alex followed as Frank pulled into the long dirt driveway. Outside the barn were a half-dozen men standing guard. Sam watched as one of the men went back inside, leaving the rest to stop them from entering the barn.

Alex pulled to a stop. All the men jumped out of the two vehicles and stood together for a moment. Before anyone could speak, a van sped around the barn from the other side. Joshua spun around to look at it. He froze when his eyes met the familiar face of Lucius. "The Fallen Immortals are getting away!" he exclaimed.

Sam's hackles rose. "Is Payton with them?"

Joshua shook his head as the van disappeared down the driveway, leaving a cloud of dust. "I'm still picking up her energy. She's inside."

Frank quickly stepped toward the group of guards, "Let's take care of these guys first."

The guards began their assault on the rescue team. Sam and the others didn't hesitate. Sam fought one man while the rest of the team neutralized those remaining.

INSIDE THE BARN, PAYTON turned her attention to the man cowering on his knees in front of her. Part of her wanted to rip the guy's head off for what Lucius had just put her through.

"You," she screamed at the man. "What the hell did you think you were doing helping him?" She focused her energy and went into his mind, looking for answers about where Lucius might have gone.

The man's hands flew to his ears as he cried out in pain. His mind yielded no helpful information. Payton stormed over and stood next to him, striking his back with her foot until he was on all fours.

"Tell me where Lucius has gone?" she asked through gritted teeth.

The man only grunted.

She booted him until he fell to the floor, splayed out. Reaching down, she picked the man up by his collar, raising her fist to strike him.

"Payton. That's enough," Joshua yelled as he entered the barn.

Her head jerked a little to the side, but it didn't register that the voice was her father's. She turned back to stare down at the whimpering man. Her jaw tightened as she punched him hard in the face until his nose bled. He went limp in her hands.

"Payton. Stop." Joshua rushed over, coming around to face her.

Payton snapped out of her fury and dropped the man to the floor, stepping back. It barely registered with her when Joshua's jaw dropped. Wiping hair off her brow with her forearm, she looked over her shoulder to see Sam and Mark had entered the barn. Their faces betrayed their shock and horror. The fog of anger faded as recognition fully set in. Her heart ached at the sight of Sam's face.

Everyone was silent as they all gaped at the surrounding scene. Bodies were strewn throughout the barn; many were unconscious while others were not so lucky.

Joshua's eyes moved to Brian's body, then hovered over the burned carcass several feet in front of them. His brows knitted.

Payton backed away, suddenly feeling parched. She rubbed her hands down her sides while her chest continued to heave. She opened her mouth to speak but found she didn't have the words to explain what had just happened.

Frank ran into the barn, stopping when he saw no one was moving. His eyes widened as he took in the sheer number of casualties. Putting his hands on his hips, he strolled to where Payton and Joshua stood.

His voice was gentle. "Alex is calling for backup. I came to see how many vans we need to take away suspects."

He turned his gaze to Payton.

Payton averted Frank's gaze as guilt enveloped her. She shook her head when she saw Sam and Mark remained frozen where they were standing.

Turning toward the side door, she ran from the barn without looking back.

JOSHUA WATCHED HIS daughter run from the barn. Dread flooded his body at what he had just witnessed.

Payton's eyes were black when he looked into them. The indigo eyes that she inherited from him were gone. Only when she realized where she was and what she was doing did they change back to their usual colour.

A vein of shock ran through him at the sight of Payton's bloody clothes and bruised body. It was unclear whether they resulted from Lucius or her own fury when taking out those around her.

Even knowing that she would soon be healed, it still pained him to see the damage inflicted on her.

Frank looked at Joshua in silence. Joshua knew Payton could have valuable information about Lucius and his plans. He also knew she needed some time to adjust to the immense power she had allowed to course through her. He worried that no one else would understand what she was going through and feared they would judge her or be afraid of her.

Sam and Mark approached and stood next to Frank. "We need to find out where Lucius has gone," said Frank.

Joshua nodded. "Give her a minute. This may not be the best time to debrief her."

Sam let out a jagged breath. "What did they... do to her? Is she going to be okay?" Sam stammered.

Joshua could see he was struggling with his emotions. "Lucius tried to turn her. My guess is he wanted her to join him."

Sam cursed, then glanced toward the body on the floor against one wall.

"Brian," he growled. "I wish I could have got my hands on him."

"The vans will be here soon. Let's take care of things here," Frank said to Mark.

The two men walked away.

Joshua stepped closer to Sam, speaking in a hushed tone, "I know you care a great deal about my daughter. That is why I must tell you, Payton is going to need you now more than ever. I am worried about her ability to control the Immortal fury within her. You mean a lot to her, and her affection for you may be what keeps her in the light. We can't lose her to shadow, Sam."

Sam stood tall, his jaw set. "Just tell me how I can help her."

CHAPTER SEVENTEEN

RUFUS, THE GINGER-HAIRED security guard, entered the elevator, taking it down to the third level. A guard stood at the entrance to the jail area. The Fallen Immortal approached the man.

"I am here to take the woman. She is to be interrogated," he said in a booming voice.

The guard looked bewildered. "I was told she is too dangerous to remove from the cell. Who gave this order?" he asked, eyeing Rufus.

Rufus took a step forward. "I did," he said, grabbing the man and twisting his head before dropping him to the floor.

He strode to the cell that housed Nadia and opened it with his key card.

Nadia sauntered over to him and placed her hand on his chest. "I thought you would never get here," she whispered before kissing Rufus hard on the mouth. When she stepped back, she asked, "Any problems upstairs?"

Rufus inhaled, then sighed. "There may be one... An Immortal Guardian is here. He has gone to find Payton. We have little time. The others will meet us outside. There is a van waiting. I will text everyone inside to tell them the raid has begun."

The pair hurried from the jail area and headed to the elevator.

A HALF DOZEN OF LUCIUS'S spies within the agency approached the vault with the librarian's key card in hand. Knowing that the key card was their only way into the vault, they knew they had to hurry before anyone noticed.

Each person grabbed as many items from the shelves as they could carry. Rushing back to the elevator, they hurried up to the surface to meet Rufus and Nadia at the getaway van.

Nadia stood next to the van as the items were placed inside. "Where's the palm stone?" she asked eagerly.

Each of the thieves looked at one another with blank expressions.

"Well? Who has it?" she insisted. She was met with silence. "You idiots! That's what you were supposed to be looking for. What good is all this junk? We need the palm stone," she barked.

"Yes, ma'am. We'll go," said a man and woman dressed in maintenance uniforms.

"Hurry.... Someone block the elevator door as soon as they come back up," she yelled as she got into the van. The rest of the thieves jumped into the van with their stolen items. One of the thieves followed the two volunteers that left to retrieve the palm stone.

Rufus's phone rang. He could see it was Lucius calling him. "What is it?" he asked.

"Get out of there. Now," Lucius hollered.

Rufus hung up the phone. "We're leaving," he announced as he jumped into the driver's seat.

"But the palm stone? Lucius will be furious if we don't retrieve it. It's part of the plan," Nadia insisted.

"It's too late for that," said Rufus as the van squealed out of the Sylvan Falls Museum parking lot and headed toward downtown.

BRYCE WAS RETURNING to his desk when he noticed a couple of staff members huddled, talking in hushed tones with one another. His super-sensitive hearing caught the word *vault*. He could tell something was happening, and they were attempting to hide it. He walked over to investigate. "What's going on over here?"

A staff member turned off her computer monitor as he approached.

"Why is your monitor off? What are you hiding?" He reached across the desk, urging the staff member to move so he could get to the monitor. The female staff member jumped on Bryce, taking him by surprise.

Her supernatural ability was evidently not strength. Instead, her body instantly grew into an impenetrable exoskeleton. Bryce fought back, finally subduing her with the help of another staff member, who then restrained her.

He flicked her desk monitor back on, only to see the empty corridor outside the vault area. "I have a horrible feeling about this," he muttered; going to his desk, he pulled up all camera feeds in the building. The cameras at the main entrance to the building, along with the jail cell area and several others, had been turned off.

Cursing, he triggered the alarm to announce that The Agency was under attack.

Still unsure exactly what was happening, he picked up his phone to use the internal announcement system. "Attention all staff. Headquarters has been breached by outsiders. No one leaves the building. If you are loyal to The Agency, please report to Operations we need to re-secure the facility."

He hung up the phone as someone took a swipe at him with a chair, narrowly missing him. Other employees were now fighting one another while more staff ran into Ops, presumably to assist him.

He entered the fray in an attempt to subdue those launching the attack against The Agency. He was baffled by how this could happen and why?

More staff members continued to enter Ops, with several burly men going directly to Bryce. "How can we help?" one of the muscle-bound men asked.

"Get down to the weapons locker and secure it. No one goes inside without my authorization. Got it?" Bryce ordered.

CHAPTER EIGHTEEN

THREE HUGE VANS SHOWED up at the farm to take suspects into custody. Medical teams had been dispatched to help the injured while the coroner and her team removed the dead. Frank and several other Agents scoured the farmhouse for any clues about Lucius and his plans.

No one had approached Payton since she ran from the barn. She was relieved not to have to speak. What could she say? Once again, she had used her extraordinary power to destroy.

Standing in the field next to the farmhouse, her mind cleared, and a feeling of calm blanketed her. Payton hugged herself and stared blankly at the area in front of her. Questions rose in her mind. Was the abduction part of her destiny?

If she had decided to join Lucius, would she still have to wield the sword?

Had Lucius won because Payton killed people?

Was she now essentially a Fallen Immortal?

"Payton?"

Payton was pulled from her thoughts by the sound of Sam's voice as he approached her from behind. She lowered her head, squeezing her eyes shut, unable to look him in the eye after everything that she'd done. She couldn't bear to see the disappointment in his eyes.

Sam moved around to stand in front of her. His auric field mingled with hers, and she knew he was standing very close. Payton slowly opened her eyes when he placed a finger under her chin, raising it.

Their eyes met, and a flood of emotions filled her. A lump filled her throat when Sam's eyes flashed with anguish. His fingers tenderly touched her cheek.

"Who did this?" his voice was thick with emotion.

"Lucius didn't like it when I refused to join him."

With delicate fingers, he examined her eyes and face. She guessed that there was still some visible bruising to be seen.

A low, angry rumble emitted from deep inside Sam.

Payton shrugged. "I'm okay." A brief silence followed as she lowered her eyes.

Sam unexpectedly pulled her into his arms, holding her close. His embrace only reminded her of how much she didn't deserve him.

Tears filled her eyes as Payton clung to him, holding tight. "Sam," she sobbed.

He murmured in her ear as he smoothed her hair. "I'm so sorry for all of this."

Tears streamed down her cheeks and onto Sam's shirt. He continued to hold her as she cried. Payton dropped her arms and pulled away from his embrace when she regained some of her composure, taking a step back.

Looking Sam in the eye, she asked, "Are you disappointed in me for losing control back there?"

Sam carefully smoothed some hair from her cheek. "You could never disappoint me. I was just surprised that you had taken on so many people. I thought I'd seen you angry, but this was something else."

Payton sniffed, bowing her head. "Oh."

Sam leaned his head close to hers. "It changes nothing between us. I don't think any less of you," he whispered.

She cocked her head. "Are you sure?"

Sam put his hand to her cheek and rubbed her face tenderly with his thumb. "I am sure," he beamed.

Payton's spirits lifted. The one person she could trust more than anyone else in the world was Sam. He was the only one who had not let her down or lied to her.

She couldn't help but fall for such a wonderful man. Though she could not yet bring herself to tell him how she felt. With so much work still ahead of her, she didn't want to endanger him again.

Sam's eyes searched hers, and she knew there was more he wanted to say.

Feeling self-conscious, she moved away from him and looked over at the crowd of people outside the barn. Payton blew out a puff of air, shoving her hands in her pockets. "I guess I better explain what happened with Lucius."

People were still milling about, but the vans were loaded and ready to leave.

Joshua and Frank were having what looked like a serious discussion as Payton and Sam approached them. Both men turned to look at them, their faces creased with worry. Payton's mind felt clear, and with Sam at her side, she felt as though everything might actually be okay.

Standing in front of Joshua and Frank, a thought struck her, and she smacked her palm to her forehead.

"Damn it," she exclaimed.

"What?" Joshua asked.

Payton pressed her hands to her cheeks. "The guard at HQ. The one working today. He's the one that called Lucius to say you were on your way. He's a Fallen Immortal."

Frank looked around at the people on the scene and back at Payton.

"Did he tell you who else is working for him?"

Payton slid her hands to her hips and shook her head. "Not exactly, but I need to tell you both what his plans are."

When Payton finished explaining what had happened with Lucius, Joshua stepped up, studying her face. “You know, this is not over,” he said.

Payton looked up at him, letting out a small laugh. “Funny. That’s exactly what Lucius said.”

Placing a hand on her upper back, Frank smiled. “I’m glad we got you back and that you are okay.”

Payton bit her lip. She felt the farthest thing from OK. She had taken lives. Again. Perhaps this was what Lucius had been aiming for? She pressed her lips into a grimace.

FRANK SENT WORD AROUND that everyone should head back to headquarters. Sam and Payton joined Frank and Joshua for the ride back. The convoy of vehicles reached the Sylvan Falls Museum parking lot at the same time.

The SUV pulled to a stop. All eyes went to the Museum building in front of them when they heard an alarm resounding. The colour drained from Frank’s face. He didn’t notice that one van carrying suspects turned and left the parking lot.

“What *is* that?” asked Sam, looking a little wide-eyed.

“The Agency’s been breached. I am the only one with access when there is a lockdown, but we better move!” Frank bolted toward the front door of the building, with Joshua, Payton, and Sam close behind him.

When they reached the drapes that usually hid the elevator room, a security guard was nowhere to be found. The elevator was propped open, and the curtain pulled back.

“This doesn’t look good,” Sam frowned.

Frank shook his head. "We need to get to the weapons locker," he announced, opening a hidden panel near the elevator, used only in emergencies such as this. Frank entered a code and waited. A robotic voice spoke. "Retinal scan commencing now."

A small screen popped out from the wall at eye height. Frank moved his face closer to it, so it could scan his eye. A second or two later, the automatic voice instructed him again as it put forward a hand-sized flat screen a little lower down. "Place your palm on the panel, Frank White."

Out of the corner of his eye, he saw Payton and Sam exchange a look of surprise.

"The elevator is now operational," the voice stated.

Joshua had already moved the piece of furniture blocking the elevator door and was standing inside, waiting. Frank joined him, then turned to face Payton, handing her his key card. "I need you to get to the library and vault. Make sure it's secured... And check that Greg is okay."

Payton looked confused. "Aren't we all going down in the elevator together?"

Frank nodded, realizing he was stressing more than he should be. He knew he needed to get his head together if they were going to regain control of The Agency. He felt more distressed than he had ever been. Then again, The Agency had never been under attack before.

Sam stepped inside the elevator next to him. "What do you need me to do, boss?"

"You and Joshua come with me to weapons... When the elevator opens, be ready for anything."

CHAPTER NINETEEN

ONLY A HANDFUL OF PEOPLE were in the hallway outside the elevator. They didn't appear to be causing any immediate trouble, so Payton headed to the right toward the vault and the library. She glanced back over her shoulder to see that Frank and Joshua were approaching the staff in the hallway while Sam was moving toward the firing range and weapons locker. Sam turned his head, and their eyes locked briefly.

Payton said a silent prayer that he'd be safe, then hurried to the library to check on Greg. She was about to let herself in with Frank's key card since she didn't have hers, only to find the lock had been broken.

She ran inside. "Greg!"

A muffled response reached her ears. She ran toward it only to find Greg on the floor face down, tied up and gagged. Rolling him over, she took off his gag before breaking his restraints.

"Are you okay? What happened?"

Greg rubbed his temple, trying to stand; Payton reached out to steady him as he stumbled. She led him to a nearby chair. Greg looked visibly shaken. She reached out and touched the side of his head. "Allow me to heal you."

A few moments later, Greg fidgeted, so she removed her hand.

"Tell me what happened?" Payton asked again, moving a hand to her hip.

Greg moved his hands animatedly, "I was in one aisle when I heard a loud crash. I rushed over to investigate, only to find a couple of people had busted through the door! I ran, but they caught me." His forehead furrowed. "I'm not much of a fighter, so I didn't stand a chance," he frowned. He rubbed his face with his hands before gazing back at her.

Payton paced back and forth in an attempt to keep her stress level down. "What did they say to you?"

He thrust his hands up. "They wanted my key card...to get into the vault."

She knew the vault was impenetrable without a key card. She stopped and looked at Greg. "Did you give it to them?"

Greg put his hands out to the side. "I didn't have a choice," he muttered. "I'm sorry...." He put his head in his hands.

"Stay here. Keep low." Payton ran out of the library and straight to the vault. She let herself in with Frank's key card and tuned in for anyone that may still be inside the sizeable area. It was quiet.

She hurried over to the computer to see that it was still off. Whoever had broken in hadn't used it. What were they looking for?

She walked aisle by aisle, looking for missing or broken items. The place was in disarray, and she knew items were definitely gone. Her heart pounded as she quickly thought of the one thing that Lucius would want more than anything.

Rushing to the shelf that housed Basil's palm stone, her hand flew to her mouth. "Oh, no," she said aloud.

Knowing that finding the palm stone was a priority, Payton left the vault and headed down toward the weapons locker to give the bad news to Frank and Joshua.

AFTER SEEING FRANK and Joshua in a brief scuffle with a few rogue Agents in the hall, Sam noticed two musclebound, well-armed Agents standing outside the doors to the weapons area. He approached them with caution. "What's going on here? We got back to find the place locked down?"

One man looked at Sam, recognizing him. "The insurgence against The Agency took us all by surprise."

Frank and Joshua joined them. "Did anyone gain access to the weapons before you got down here?"

"We don't know yet if anything's missing or how many of the staff have rebelled. We came down as soon as Bryce sounded the alarm. He instructed us not to let anyone in. It doesn't look like they want to kill any of us. No one has bothered us since we got here."

Sam found it odd that no one was using weapons. He glanced at Frank.

"Let's get some gear on and head to Ops," Frank advised.

Sam cursed, running his hand down his face. "I can only imagine what's happening up there."

Joshua and Frank exchanged a worried look. Joshua stood more rigid than usual. Sam watched the men's faces, realizing that Frank and Joshua were communicating with one another telepathically.

Sam moved past the guards and went to the weapons locker to get body armour and a taser, just in case. Who knew what they would be up against and what staff members he was going to have to fight? There were all kinds of supernatural beings working for The Agency. Some, more dangerous than others.

Frank joined him in the weapons area and suited up as well. Joshua stepped up. "I do not require armour. I will check out the rest of this floor for any other rogue Agents and meet you back in operations."

Frank agreed, then looked at Sam. Doing up his body armour, he frowned. "We don't know how many people we are up against here. Grab a couple of headsets so we can stay in touch."

Sam nodded and tucked a headset behind his ear, then placed the earpiece. He sniffed the air, and his mouth curved into a grin. Payton entered the room seconds later, looking frantic.

"They've got the palm stone," she blurted.

Frank's eyes became saucers. "Damn it."

WHEN THE GROUP REACHED the Operations centre, it was a mess, with overturned chairs, broken tables and smashed computer screens. Payton and the others quickly assessed the situation. Twenty or more people were fighting with one another. Payton could feel a range of emotions from the staff, almost to the point of overwhelming her.

Bryce turned to them after knocking out another staff member. Hurrying over, he rubbed some blood from his chin as he spoke. "Boy, am I happy to see you guys? It looks like someone in security has betrayed us, along with many staff members. He freed the woman we had in custody. There is no way to know who is on our side here. Everything has gone to hell quickly."

Payton's brows shot up. "Nadia?" Her jaw clenched. Lucius's plan had already begun, and it was only meant to get worse.

"Do you know where the guard and the woman are now?" asked Frank.

Bryce shook his head. "The cameras were turned off in the cells, elevator and at street level. I wouldn't have known, but I overheard staff talking about corridor cameras. I think the vault has been targeted but haven't had time to get down there myself. We were attacked as soon as I realized something was wrong." He wiped his brow.

Frank grimaced. "The vault *has* been breached. We need to re-secure the facility right away. We've got men up top and suspects that need to be processed, but that can wait until we fix things here. Get a headset on, and keep me posted."

Payton's stomach flipped when she looked over to see Alex and Mark walking toward them, both looking frazzled.

"Sir. One of the vans drivers took off with the prisoners," blurted Alex.

"The driver is probably one of Lucius's men," Payton interjected, wishing she had been able to stop Lucius from carrying out the attack. The only consolation in *her* being abducted was that Sam hadn't been hurt, and Brian was no longer a threat.

"Are the other two vans staying?" asked Frank.

Mark nodded. "The prisoners and the vans are secured for now. We came down to see if we can help here?"

Frank sighed, passing more headsets out to his Agents. "Alex, you go upstairs and stand guard in case there are any more intruders. Don't let anyone leave! Mark, you're with me. We'll check out this level first and then go floor by floor."

He turned to Payton and Sam, nodding at Payton to let her know he wanted to communicate telepathically. She opened her mind to him.

'We need to get that palm stone back. I doubt Nadia is in the building. Just find the palm stone,' he told her telepathically.

Payton spoke aloud, "I will."

Sam looked at her, his brow creased.

'Frank? Do you think the attack on The Agency was just so Lucius could get his hands on the palm stone?' Payton asked telepathically.

Frank tugged his earlobe. "I don't know. Just be on alert. We don't know who we can trust right now."

Payton motioned to Sam. "Let's go that way." She pointed.

Sam glanced sideways at her while they proceeded down the hall past offices and several meeting rooms. "Are you feeling better now that Brian is no longer a problem?" Sam asked.

Payton sensed some uncertainty from Sam. They had spoken little since they left the farm. She shrugged. "I am relieved he won't bother me again. I mean, Lucius didn't mean to kill him. If Brian hadn't been killed, Lucius was going to take me with him along with the other Immortals." She thought for a moment before adding, "I don't think Lucius was thrilled when I fought back. He was pretty pissed to find out about Joshua being here, and I'm guessing he has no clue about Azrael or the sword." She stopped and turned to face Sam. "I think I put a damper on his plans. But I don't think he'll quit wanting to rule the world. Lucius has been planning something big for a long time. This isn't his end game.... yet. I'm afraid things will get a lot worse if we don't stop the Fallen Immortals soon." Payton had a feeling that Lucius would *never* stop, which meant she would have no choice but to kill him. Which also meant wielding the sword of power. She blanched at the thought.

Sam frowned as he watched her. "What's wrong? You look worried."

Payton waved her hand dismissively. "It's nothing." She turned back toward the corridor. "Let's keep searching for any problems."

Just as Payton expected, there were no other staff fights or indications of problems from any of the rooms they had checked. In fact, most of the rooms, including the cafeteria, were nearly empty.

They made it to the infirmary without incident when Dr. Mary James rushed toward them, crying out. "Help, Sam! Someone is attacking the nurses in the infirmary!"

The doctor pushed Payton to one side and ran at Sam, launching herself at him. Sam grunted and pushed her off. He clutched at his throat immediately as blood spurted from his neck.

Payton knew he was in trouble as he fell back, his face pale and filled with panic. She grabbed the doctor and smashed her up against the wall. "Why?" Payton screamed at Doctor James, pushing her arm against the woman's throat.

"My orders were to take out Sam." Mary moved her eyes down to Sam as he continued to bleed out. She had a cruel smile on her face. "It looks as though I've accomplished my task."

Payton punched the doctor several times, knocking her out, throwing her to one side, cursing the woman.

She dropped to her knees by Sam and placed a hand on his wound. "Come on, Sam. Stay with me," she breathed as Sam's eyes closed. She tapped her earpiece with her free hand. "Frank. Sam's been stabbed," she gasped into her headset.

Payton adjusted herself on the floor and braced both her hands against Sam's wound. The bleeding slowed, but she could see he had lost a lot of blood and was unconscious. Payton heard someone running toward them. Glancing up, she saw fear in Frank and Mark's eyes as they approached. Frank knelt on the other side of Sam, putting a hand to his chest. He cast a glance at Dr. James, then back at Payton.

Payton tilted her head, gritting her teeth. "She's the one who stabbed him. She said Lucius wants him gone."

Her fear that Sam was in danger of dying fueled her hatred for Lucius all the more. She knew Lucius wanted Sam out of the way, hoping that the loss would send Payton over the edge.

Payton didn't doubt that it would destroy her. A life without Sam wasn't something she could afford to entertain. Payton could see that Sam's wound had closed. She reached for his wrist, checking for a pulse. Closing her eyes, she sighed when she found one.

"He's going to need a blood transfusion or to rest until his blood levels come back up. But I think he'll be okay." She stood and wiped Sam's blood off her trembling hands onto her trousers, doing her best to look calm in front of Frank and Mark. Inside, she was a hot mess.

Mark had cuffed Dr. James and was standing over the woman, giving her a death stare.

"Payton!" Joshua's voice rang out as he ran toward them. He stopped when he saw Sam on the floor. He tilted his head, peering down at him. "Is he...?"

Payton choked down the urge to burst into tears. "He'll live, but we need to move him," she managed. Joshua and the others helped Payton carry Sam into the infirmary, where they placed him carefully onto a cot.

"We need some help here," Frank called out before a couple of staff members rushed over from their hiding spot. A nurse began tending to Sam right away, and Payton knew he would be in excellent hands now that Dr. James was no longer a threat.

The voices of the medical staff and Frank faded as she thought about the day she was having. Payton cursed herself for not being more psychically tuned in as she and Sam walked down the hall.

Somehow, Payton had missed Mary's energy because she was focused on other things. If she had sensed the doctor sooner, she might have saved Sam from being stabbed. Payton felt tears sting her eyes. She touched Sam's cheek, wishing it was her on the cot and not him.

She took a step back as a nurse put a thick blanket over Sam. She watched as the woman placed an I.V. into his arm to prepare for a blood transfusion.

Knowing Sam was going to be okay, her fear was replaced with anger. Payton clenched her fists. "Frank, stay with Sam. Make sure he is taken care of. Dad and I are going to find the palm stone, then we are going after Lucius," she snapped.

Joshua blinked. A look of surprise crossed his face.

"But...how will you...?" Frank blurted, looking concerned.

Joshua placed a hand on Payton's back. "Azrael is on his way. I just spoke with him before I found you in the corridor."

Payton shook her head. "I'm not waiting for someone to die while we wait for Azrael. The palm stone has been taken, and we need to get it back." She stormed out of the infirmary with Joshua on her heels.

CHAPTER TWENTY

HEADING INTO THE OPERATIONS Centre, Joshua glanced over at Payton. "Do you have any way of sensing the stone?" Joshua asked her, sounding hopeful.

Payton shook her head. "No. But if it was taken by someone here on staff, it could still be in the building." She looked around as they entered the Operations Centre.

Bryce rushed over to them as soon as he saw Payton make eye contact. "Is there anything else I can do to help?"

"Yes. Do you have any way to know who entered the vault?"

Bryce put a finger in the air, then hurried to his desk. "I have access to all key card swipes in the building." He tapped his keyboard while looking at his computer monitor.

"It was accessed twice in the last hour," he said, looking over at Payton.

She put her hands on her hips. "Is there a camera in there?"

Bryce nodded. "There is a camera in the hallway. Let's check it." Bryce tapped his keyboard, pulling up the feeds of all cameras that were still working. He quickly located the camera in the hall outside the vault and scrolled through the latest footage, then stopped. "Here!" He pointed at the screen. "These two seem to be the most recent people to enter." Examining the footage, he paused it when the couple reappeared in the hallway.

"Do you recognize them?" Joshua asked him.

Bryce's lips turned down. "I don't know them. But they are wearing maintenance uniforms. If that helps?"

Payton gazed at Bryce. "Have you seen them today?"

"No. But the hallway cameras should show which way they went." He forwarded through the hallway footage to see the pair headed down to the third floor.

"Why are they headed to the jail cells?" Payton was surprised. The footage showed that the man and woman entered the cell area but were quickly shooed away by armed staff. She pointed at the screen. "What time was this footage recorded?"

Bryce checked and looked at her. "Half-hour ago. They are still in the building."

Payton swore. "I must have just missed them when I went into the vault. Can you see where they went?"

Again, Bryce looked at the video before responding. "They appear to still be on level three. I don't see them having entered the elevators."

"What about the stairwells? Can they access those?" asked Payton.

"No. When there is an attack on HQ, the whole place locks down. Everything has been locked since I discovered the breach. Only Frank can restore access to the stairwells or the elevator. I am sure they are still below ground," Bryce insisted.

Payton and Joshua nodded, knowing that the last people to leave HQ likely had blocked the elevator, so the door wouldn't close.

"Let's go find them," said Payton, heading for the elevator.

PAYTON AND JOSHUA STEPPED into the hallway on level 3, only to encounter utter silence. There appeared to be no one around, but Payton felt otherwise. She reached out with her psychic senses, discovering a couple of people hiding in a server room a short distance away.

She communicated with her father telepathically, letting him know where the suspects were. 'I'll go in first. We'll fan off in different directions once we are inside.'

Joshua nodded a couple of times. As they approached the door, they realized it required a passcode. Frank's key card would not work. Payton put her hand up to the panel, sending a surge of electrical energy, shorting it out. The door popped open.

Joshua looked at her with a dubious expression.

Payton shrugged, putting her hands out to the side. "What? There's no other way in," she whispered, knowing that she had just damaged an expensive piece of tech.

Pushing the door completely open, she stepped inside the vast space with heightened senses, unsure of what to expect. The air-conditioned room felt a couple of degrees cooler than the hallway had. The white noise of the room's fans muted some of the other sounds in the room.

Neon blue and yellow lights flickered on each of the tall futuristic-looking servers. Several long rows of machines stretched through the space.

Looking around, Payton didn't see anyone right away. Going row by row, she tuned in, looking for anyone aside from her and Joshua. It didn't take long to locate the pair. Payton called out to Joshua in her mind to let him know where they were hiding.

Joshua went down and around them on one side while Payton moved directly in front of them. The female, a short and stocky woman, charged Payton.

Bending her arm, Payton used her elbow to knock the woman onto her butt, then reached for the woman's collar, pulling her up. "Where's the palm stone?" Payton asked.

The woman stared at her with a blank expression. Payton shook her. "Where is it?" The woman didn't fight back or acknowledge Payton's question. Payton probed the woman's mind for information. The woman appeared unaware that Payton was reading her thoughts until her head began hurting.

"Stop!" the woman cried out.

Payton gritted her teeth. "I know you have the palm stone. Give it to me, and you won't be hurt."

Letting her guard down for a moment, Payton cast her sights on a man several feet away. He was watching Payton with narrowed eyes. "Don't hurt her," he ordered.

"Then hand over the palm stone," Payton demanded.

Before the man could answer or move, Joshua rounded the corner and tackled him from behind. Joshua's eyes widened as he watched Payton. "Watch out," he yelled.

A sharp pain tore through Payton's leg. She yelped, releasing her grasp on the suspect. Looking down, she saw a small dagger in the woman's hands. She grabbed it and tossed it aside. Wincing, Payton put her hand over the wound to staunch the bleeding.

The woman scrambled to get away, but Payton lunged at her, grabbing her clothing. She punched the woman, knocking her out.

Joshua held the male suspect, putting him in a sleeper hold and carefully easing the man to the floor. He looked over at Payton and chided, "you don't always have to hit people to knock them out."

Payton made a face and searched the woman's pockets. Using the same hand she'd used to heal her leg wound, she felt something smooth against her fingertips. She glanced at Joshua. "I think I've got it."

Reaching further into the woman's pocket, her hands clutched the palm stone. She felt it immediately heat up in her hand as she pulled it out to look at it. Unexpectedly, the stone vibrated. Payton's jaw dropped.

"Get it out of the room. Now!" Joshua threw his arm out to the side, pointing at the exit.

Payton hurried for the door, barely making it into the hallway before the palm stone exploded into a million pieces. Payton turned away as it shattered, shielding her eyes.

Joshua was standing next to her within seconds. "Are you okay?" he asked, looking her over for injuries.

"I'm fine." She glanced down at her leg to see it had fully healed. "What made the stone explode?" she asked Joshua.

Joshua frowned. "Basil created the enchanted stone with blood magic. Being his granddaughter, your blood was able to destroy it."

Payton looked at her hands in shock. "The blood on my hands...?"

Joshua smiled and placed a hand on her upper back. "Yes. It would seem so."

Payton gazed at her father's kind face. "How did you know it would explode?"

He grinned back at her. "I know how blood magic works... And I did not think Frank would be very pleased if The Agency's servers were damaged. That's why I told you to run."

Payton scratched her forehead in disbelief. "Thanks for that. At least the palm stone won't be making it into Lucius's hands anytime soon." She pointed toward the room where they'd left the two suspects. "I guess we better get those two to the cells. I hope there is enough room for them."

WALKING INTO OPS TEN minutes later with her father, Payton observed the giant wall screen used to monitor cameras all over Sylvan Falls. It came to life before her eyes with a view of downtown.

Her heart dropped at what she saw.

The middle of Main Street was lined with dozens of people fighting, while others were breaking into shops and smashing the few vehicles parked nearby.

Payton flinched when, amidst the fighting, she noticed the Fallen Immortals that had held her captive. Peering closer, her gaze fixed on Lucius. He was there, fighting against supernaturals alongside the rest of his band of rebels.

Payton made a long face. "I've gotta go." She turned to march toward the elevators.

Joshua called out. "Wait. I'm coming with you."

CHAPTER TWENTY-ONE

SAM REGAINED CONSCIOUSNESS and was sitting up with his legs over the side of the cot. A nurse removed a cannula from his arm where he had received blood. At the same time, Frank just finished explaining that Payton had saved his life as Azrael entered the infirmary.

Looking troubled, the Immortal Guardian asked, "Where is Payton?"

Sam's eyes flitted to the leather-wrapped item Azrael carefully clutched in his hands, his forehead creased. Azrael had the sword of power, which meant he intended to give it to Payton. A bolt of fear struck him.

Frank answered Azrael. "She was with Joshua. Did you ask in Ops?"

Azrael looked alarmed. "A young man there told me she left. I thought she would be with you. I have to find her." He turned and started walking out of the infirmary without another word.

Sam stood. "Wait. I'm coming with you."

"It's too dangerous," Frank blurted, reaching for Sam.

Sam shoved his shoulders back, looking at Frank. "Payton has saved my life more times than I care to think about. I'll be damned if I'm going to let her face down that bastard on her own."

Azrael, who had stopped in his tracks, shook his head. "You won't last five minutes against the Fallen Immortals."

Sam squinted at Azrael. "Yeah? Watch me!" he stormed past.

In Ops, Sam and Azrael approached Bryce, who had his head down, busily working at a computer keyboard.

"Where is Payton?" asked Sam.

Bryce looked up, pausing a moment before answering. He bit his lip and pointed to the scene of downtown Sylvan Falls on the large screen. "She went there."

Sam and Azrael looked at one another in silence, then turned and stalked toward the steps to the elevator.

"We'll take my vehicle. I'm driving," Sam's deep voice grumbled.

PAYTON PULLED THE SUV over and turned off the ignition as Joshua put his hand on her arm. "We should really wait for Azrael before engaging Lucius."

Payton's eyes blazed. "He needs to pay for the damage he has caused... the lives he has taken." Her jaw tightened. "The longer we wait, the more people get hurt."

Joshua closed his eyes for a moment, then looked back at Payton. "I am worried about you facing him again."

Payton tried to still her anger at Lucius. After all, it wasn't like she wanted to fight him. But he had to be stopped. Once and for all. She could feel her father's emotions and knew he was unsure how she would fare in the upcoming battle. He wasn't alone in those thoughts. Joshua took her hand and squeezed it. "Whatever happens today. I want you to know I love you."

Payton smiled for a moment. "I love you too, dad," she called him dad for the second time that day. If everything went to hell in the next hour, she wanted him to know that she cared about him. "I'm grateful that I finally met you. I'm sorry we have had little time together." She felt a twinge of pain in her chest. This was the moment Azrael had trained her for. It was her job to stop Lucius, even though she desperately didn't want to kill anyone else.

Joshua's eyes were moist with tears, surprising Payton and filling her with compassion. He cleared his throat. "Do not speak as if you will not see me again.... When you wield the sword...."

Payton put a palm up. "*If* I wield it..." she swallowed, realizing there was no chance of escaping her destiny. It was about to play out. She felt a sense of anticipation mixed with uncertainty. What if the blade turned her into a Fallen One?

Joshua sensed her concern. "Do not allow your mind to think that. I will be at your side. You are stronger than the blade. Use it to take down our enemies. *That* is your destiny."

"But the prophecy says it is undecided what side I will land on. I don't want to become evil." Payton studied her father's face for reassurance that she would be okay.

Joshua was resolute. "You can do this and remain an Immortal Guardian. I know it."

There was nothing more to say. Payton and Joshua got out of the SUV to walk the rest of the way. She wasn't sure what exactly she hoped to do without the sword in hand. The Fallen would be immune to attack magic. She and her father would have to fight hand to hand with the Fallen Immortals.

The crowd didn't notice her and Joshua as they moved through the throng of people. Payton marched to where Lucius was holding onto a superhuman. Putting her arms out to the side, she called out, "Lucius!"

He peered over his shoulder, dropping the man he was holding. With an evil grin, he turned and walked toward her. His eyes darted to Joshua. "I see you have brought daddy with you." Lucius glared at Joshua. "It has been a long time, brother," he spat.

Joshua looked at Lucius with contempt. "I am not your brother. You lost the right to call me that long ago. Your brief reign of terror ends today, Lucius." Joshua's voice was unwavering.

The corner of Lucius's mouth lifted in a smirk. "I do not think so. What do you hope to do? There are six of us and only two of you. Not to mention my army of supernatural beings."

Joshua didn't look bothered by Lucius's remarks. "If you come peacefully, no one else needs to die today."

Lucius laughed.

Payton clenched her fists. With her unwavering Immortal power intensifying, she knew she was ready to take down her enemy. Her inner voice whispered to her to attack the man that had killed her family.

She noticed several of the Fallen Immortals, including Nadia, approaching them. Joshua gave a slight nod with a side glance at Payton before rushing at one of the Fallen Immortals. The two men began fighting. The rest of the Fallen Immortals were quickly distracted by multiple supernaturals attacking them.

"Sylvan Falls is mine. It is time for you to join the rest of your Fallen Immortal family or suffer," said Lucius, looking at Payton.

"You are not my family," Payton spat through caged teeth.

She rushed at Lucius at full speed, kicking him with enough force to send him flying backward. Lucius staggered momentarily, then charged Payton. She dodged a punch and jumped back a couple of steps.

They both circled one another in a fighting stance.

Each time Payton and Lucius got close to one another, Payton threw a punch at him. Lucius blocked her blows, striking her hard a couple of times.

She landed a solid blow to his left cheek. He rubbed it gingerly, his nostrils flared. "If you will not join me, I will make sure that you suffer." He threw several more punches her way.

Payton dodged some of them and blocked the others. "I told you, I will not join you." She took several steps back, adjusting her stance and taking a quick glance at the surrounding scene. Her father was holding his own, but who knew for how long?

The lovely town that she had come to call home was being destroyed by evil, and she had to stop it. "I am not afraid of you. You can't hurt me."

The Fallen Immortal's lips drew back in a snarl. "Maybe not. But I can destroy everyone that you love.... Then you will join me." He had a look of satisfaction on his face at Payton's reaction.

She thought of Sam and how Lucius had tried to have him killed. Payton became enraged, raising her fist to strike another blow. Lucius laughed as he blocked her punch.

Payton tried a roundhouse kick, only for him to block the kick with his arm.

Lucius threw a counter punch, and Payton was able to grab his arm, twisting it at an unnatural angle behind his back.

Lucius kicked backward at her leg so she'd release him.

Payton winced, letting him go and stepping away. Lucius spun around, resuming eye contact.

Payton stepped up, attempting a quick uppercut that connected. His head flew back. He reciprocated by grabbing her shoulder in a vice-like grip and punching her in the face.

She leaned forward slightly and thrust her knee to his stomach.

Lucius reeled and took a step back. His eyes were black with rage. With a sudden movement, he grabbed her by her shirt. Payton bent her arm, using her elbow to bash his jaw, followed by a left hook. Lucius sidestepped, blocking the blow while grabbing her arm simultaneously. He pulled her arm forward and, with his palm, struck the top of her shoulder; then, with a sweep of his leg, Lucius flung her to the ground.

Straddling her, he dropped to his knees, punching her in rapid succession.

Payton tried but failed to fight him off. She kicked and grabbed at him but could not stop him from hitting her, nor could she throw him off.

She recognized the fury in him as the very same one she struggled against each time she lost her temper. He would not stop in this state of mind.

She knew *she* wouldn't if the tables were turned.

CHAPTER TWENTY-TWO

THE SOUNDS OF CHANTING filled the air as Di, Margret, and Therrien marched toward the crowded Main Street with close to two thousand elemental witches and warlocks. When they were close enough to the battle, they raised their arms in unison, casting a sleeping spell over all those affected by magic. All supernatural beings within their sights fell to the ground, except, of course, the witches and warlocks themselves.

Only Immortal Guardians and Fallen Immortals were still standing among them.

Di and Margret looked on in horror as Lucius pounded on Payton ceaselessly. Her brown hair splayed around her bloodied and bruised face. Payton flailed, then stopped, appearing to give up. With Lucius sitting over Payton, she couldn't move.

"Stop it," screamed Di, running toward them, hoping they weren't too late.

Lucius took no notice of anyone, including Di. His eyes were black with fury as he hit Payton again and again. Di stepped to one side, tears filling her eyes as she watched, helpless.

NEARLY EVERY HEREDITARY witch and warlock in Sylvan Falls was blocking the street. Sam pushed his way through the crowd with Azrael next to him, holding the sword. He was shocked to see Margret and an older man that he didn't know heading toward the group.

Her eyes bulged when she saw Azrael at Sam's side. "You've returned?" she asked, looking concerned.

Azrael pressed his lips in a slight grin, disregarding her question. "What's happened to everyone?" he asked, looking around at the mass of bodies on the ground.

She motioned to her small army of witches. "We have cast a sleeping spell over everyone that was within our line of sight."

Sam looked around. Joshua appeared to be holding his own, fighting off several Immortals. Sam and Azrael both caught sight of Payton at that exact moment. Sam groaned, and his heart sank at the sight of Lucius beating Payton. She appeared to be barely conscious and was not fighting back.

Without taking the time to undress, Sam shifted into his bear form and rushed at Lucius.

Before he could get to him, Nadia and another of the Fallen Immortals ran at Sam-bear.

Growling ferociously, he scratched and bit at them. Attempting to go after one of them at a time, each time he jumped at one of them, the other would kick or punch him from behind, fueling his anger.

AZRAEL WENT INTO ACTION right away, carefully unwrapping the hilt of the sword of power. Standing about ten feet from Payton, he called to her telepathically. 'Payton. Reach out and take the sword. It's in my hands.'

Payton responded, her voice in his head. 'I can't see you.'

Azrael shifted his stance. 'I am behind Lucius and to your right. Just reach out with your mind. You will feel the sword.'

FEELING EXHAUSTED, Payton thrashed at the pavement again with closed fists until it cracked beneath them. She admonished herself as her mind raced. *He's beating me to death, and I can't do a damn thing!*

She wondered how long it would be before she would succumb to the painful pounding.

Unaware of anything except the searing pain in her body and face, she was startled when she heard Azrael's voice in her head. Fear snaked through her.

What if the blade turns me? The thought was fleeting, and she was growing weaker by the minute. She had to stop Lucius.

Closing her eyes, she concentrated on the sword in Azrael's hands. It was calling to her with a low hum. She felt it connecting with her.

Payton angled her head just enough to see the hilt poking out of the leather wrapping that Azrael was holding in his hands. Thrusting her hand out to the side, the sword flew through the air and into her palm at a rapid speed.

Holding the handle, she used its pommel to smash Lucius in the head. He fell to one side, and she was able to roll away from him.

Jumping to her feet, she turned to see Lucius was also back on his feet, looking dazed. She felt her body vibrate in sync with the sword. Her power was magnified, making her feel invincible. Her body now glowed in a golden light, wholly healed. Everyone around her stood frozen, watching her.

Lucius staggered backward, eyes wide. For the first time, Payton saw he was genuinely afraid.

"It can't be?" Lucius stammered.

Seeing Di standing within reach, without warning, he grabbed her. Putting his arm around her, he pulled her against him, using Di as a shield while threatening, "I'll kill her!"

"The hell you will," bellowed Payton. Taking the sword's hilt into both hands, she took two quick steps forward and swung at Lucius.

He dropped Di to the ground seconds before the sword swung over Di's head, missing her entirely. She crawled away to safety. Lucius's head hit the ground before his body fell, then instantly, it all turned to ash.

Payton turned ninety degrees to the left and saw the horrified faces of the other Fallen Ones. The sword vibrated in her hands, summoning her to finish her task. '*Kill them!*' It ordered.

Losing herself to the power within her and the blade, Payton thrust the bloodied sword into the air. With a loud roar, she ran at the Fallen Ones, smiting each one down before they could flee. Ash filled the air, then settled slowly to the ground.

Barely registering what she had done and shaking violently, Payton finally glanced at the panic-stricken faces of those around her.

The ground quaked as large cracks appeared on the pavement. Sparks from overhead power lines flashed. Alarms sounded from shops and nearby cars.

Payton's chest heaved as beams of light blasted out of her. The intensity of the sword left her in awe. The sword continued to whisper, 'Kill them, kill them all.'

She searched the crowd for her father. Finding him, tears filled her eyes.

Payton dropped the blade, and its sharpened tip pierced the asphalt with a flash of light, then wobbled slowly. Her body continued to vibrate, albeit less noticeably. Her hands flew to her head.

"Stop." She screamed.

Azrael and Joshua ran to either side of her in an instant. Joshua placed a hand on her back while Azrael touched her shoulder.

"What is it? What is wrong?" Joshua scanned her face.

She faced her father. "The sword. It's calling to me. It's not finished." She put a hand to her face. "Don't you see? It will never be finished.... I can't do this," she cried, shaking her head.

Joshua rubbed her back with one hand, his voice soothing. "What do you need me to do?"

"Take it. Hide it somewhere where I can't find it," Payton whimpered.

Her head dropped. The awareness of what had unfolded was seeping into her bones. The guilt that accompanied it started its slow torture of her mind and soul.

Joshua took the leather cloth from Azrael and deftly used it to pick up the sword, wrapping it. He walked it over to Azrael, handing it to him. Azrael took it without saying a word. Both men gazed at her with compassion.

Payton ran her hands through her hair and smoothed it back over her shoulders. Her thoughts went to Sam. She was sure she'd seen Sam-bear run past her while Lucius was beating her. Or maybe she had just felt his presence? Turning in a circle, she looked for him, praying he was not injured too badly. *Where is he?* She felt a swell of panic when she couldn't see him right away.

"Sam!" she called out, continuing to walk around looking for him.

His voice rang out. "I'm here." Sam ran toward her with his shirt still unbuttoned.

"Thank God," she cried as he reached her, and she enveloped him in a hug.

Sam winced. "Easy," he laughed.

Payton let go, taking a step back. "Are you okay?" she asked, raising her brows.

Sam grinned. "I have a few sore ribs, but I'll live."

"Where were you? Where did you go?" she blinked.

Sam bit his lip. "When I saw you taking care of those Fallen Immortals. I thought it better to shift into my human form back at the car, so I ran to grab a spare change of clothing before coming to find you." He motioned to himself with his hands.

Without further thought, Payton placed a gentle hand against his bare skin. "I'll heal your ribs for you."

Sam grinned and carefully removed her hand. "Let's not do this here," he said, looking red-faced.

Payton looked around to realize that many grinning faces were watching them.

CHAPTER TWENTY-THREE

THE CROWD OF WITCHES and warlocks dispersed, with Margret and several elder council members approaching Payton.

"Thank you for your help today," said Payton to the group of witches.

A mature, pleasant-looking man put a hand out to Payton. "My name is Therrien. As a member of the Elders' council, I want to offer my gratitude to you. You have helped dispense of the evil that has plagued this town for too long. Maybe our lives can finally go back to normal." The man bowed his head.

Margret stood next to him, looking unsure of what to say. Therrien motioned to her. "Margret. I believe you have something to say to this woman?"

Payton interrupted, looking at Therrien with a slight smile. "Payton. My name is Payton."

Therrien nodded and looked at Margret again.

Margret cleared her throat. "I am truly sorry for my treatment of you. I misjudged you." The Supreme Elder looked sincere.

Payton shoved her hands in her pockets and bobbed her head in silence.

Di, who had been observing her, stepped up and put a hand on her arm. "Are you okay? You look a little out of sorts."

"I will be. At least it's over." Payton gave a half shrug and frowned.

"If there is ever anything you need?" offered Margret.

Payton pulled a hand from her pocket and gestured toward her. "There is one thing. Please reconsider allowing other witches to join The Agency. We could really use their skills. I, for one, would appreciate the help on some cases."

Margret put a finger to her lips and looked at her fellow council members. Therrien and the others exchanged a knowing look before Margret answered. "I believe that can be arranged."

Payton pressed her lips into a smile. "If you will excuse me, we have an Agency to re-secure."

IT WASN'T MUCH LONGER before the people on the street and sidewalks stirred. They stood looking disoriented and confused. When most had regained their senses, Azrael stood before them.

Many were awestruck at the sight of him. People in the town were just finding out that one of the town's founders was an Immortal.

"To those of you who may not know who I am, my name is Azrael Sylvan. I am a founder of this great town. I don't know how many of you sided with the Immortal that many called Master. Those who have done so will be disappointed to learn that he is gone. He and the others like him were struck down today. I am here to tell you that your attempts at an uprising will not happen today or any other day."

"Sylvan Falls is a safe place for all paranormal and supernatural beings. Where all of us are equal and fairly treated. If any of you cannot or will not honour this, we ask that you leave our town and make your way elsewhere. You are no longer welcome here."

"We have zero tolerance for any crimes against one another, no matter who you are. No exceptions. You will be taken into custody and imprisoned if you cause any trouble. Is there anyone here who wishes to speak?"

The voices within the crowd began as a low hum before several loud voices stood out.

"What happened? Master promised us we could run the town the way we wanted," a female voice echoed.

"He lied to all of you. He told you what you needed to hear so that he could control you," Azrael announced.

Several people stepped forward and thanked Azrael for helping them.

"Does this mean there will be no more murders of supernaturals?" asked one young man.

Azrael nodded.

A few crowd members pushed others around.

Without hesitation, nearby warlocks and witches cast spells to hold them in place until they could be rounded up and removed from the area.

"What about the humans that left town? Will they be able to come back?" asked one sad-looking woman. Azrael pressed his lips into a frown. "I am afraid the spell that protects our town from outsiders will remain."

"If the master is dead, where is his body?" asked a skeptical voice in the crowd.

"The Fallen Ones have turned to dust. They are no more," Azrael stated.

Azrael clutched the leather-wrapped sword to his side, hoping that no one would challenge him or try to touch the blade.

The sword's effect on Payton was a shock to him, and he wanted to get the blade locked away somewhere safe as soon as possible.

As he turned to leave, he noticed Payton watching him out of the corner of her eye. He wondered if wielding the sword would have any long-lasting adverse effects on her.

Someday he would tell her more of what he knew about the sword, but for now, Payton was free to live her life as she saw fit. Her destiny had been fulfilled.

CHAPTER TWENTY-FOUR

BACK AT THE AGENCY Headquarters, Frank was finally making headway to determine which staff members had betrayed The Agency versus those who remained loyal.

With the jail cells full to bursting, he began preparing to have the criminals shipped off to The Agency's prison in the Yukon Territories.

There they would be dealt with according to the crimes they committed. Rehabilitation was always the first goal.

Frank knew Lucius had lied to people, promising them they would have more control over their lives once he rose to power. They didn't stop to appreciate that they lived in a town where supernatural beings had more rights and freedoms than anywhere else. Sylvan Falls was one of a handful of places where superhumans and other supernatural beings did not have to hide who they were.

Frank personally sat down to interrogate as many suspects as possible. He needed to understand why and how such an attack could happen.

Dr. Mary James proved to be the most forthcoming once she knew that Lucius and the other Fallen Immortals in town were dead.

"The idea was to keep everyone busy here at headquarters while Lucius and his people took care of those in town that resisted him," she admitted.

"Why did you try to kill Sam?" Frank asked.

"His death was intended to send Payton into a state of despair, resulting in her becoming evil, or so Lucius thought. Personally, I would have preferred to keep Sam for myself… but…." She looked past Frank with a tasteless grin.

Frank rolled his eyes. "What about the vault? What do you know about what was taken?"

The doctor shrugged. "We each had our own individual missions. I know nothing about the vault."

When Frank moved on to another former staff member who knew about the vault thefts, he was disappointed with the lack of information the suspect gave him.

"We were told to find a green palm stone. I don't know what the item was for," said the man Frank was interrogating.

"Tell me what items were removed from the vault?" Frank insisted.

The suspect shook his head and shrugged. "I can't help with that."

Suspect after suspect claimed to have no knowledge of what was taken. This left Frank to believe that the people who took the items had not been caught. Which meant the stolen artifacts were still out there and could cause a lot of problems.

All those who had been arrested would never be welcome again at The Agency as staff members. They would remain on The Agency's watch list if they were ever released from custody.

He was glad that there had only been one employee death, though he would have preferred none. Aside from the massive cleanup in the Operations Centre, there was significant damage to the second and third levels of the underground facility. It would take time to repair and clean up. Not to mention hiring and vetting new staff, including a new doctor. Frank leaned against one of the desks in Operations and sighed.

"What a mess," he mumbled as the elevator doors opened to the Operations platform.

He turned to see three Immortal Guardians and Sam.

Walking over to meet them, he took in the sight of Payton, noticing how haunted she looked. He wondered what had happened but knew now wasn't the time to ask for details.

"I assume it's over?" Frank asked.

Azrael nodded and motioned to the wrapped sword. "We need to secure this."

Frank scoffed. "We need to secure this entire place. Locks have been broken throughout the facility. The lock is still working fine for the vault, but it's been pillaged. I must arrange new codes and key cards. I have no idea how many items have been taken aside from the palm stone. It looks bad down there."

Azrael's expression was grim. "That is cause for concern."

"I have guards down there, but we need Payton," urged Frank. He looked at Payton. "When you are up to it, I will have you check the inventory against what is down there. You know the vault better than anyone."

Payton's brows drew together. "I can start right away."

Azrael's eyes went to Payton. "Take your time. You have just had tremendous power course through you, unlike anything I've ever seen. It is good to get some rest before taking on anything new."

Payton shrugged. Her eyes went to the sword in Azrael's hands, then to the floor.

Azrael's voice softened. "I will hide the sword. There is a hidden section within the vault that will safely secure it."

"I didn't know that," said Payton, looking up at Azrael.

Frank watched Payton's face. "It's only accessible by Azrael. That's why I never mentioned it. You won't find it unless you know where to look," said Frank.

PAYTON GLANCED AT SAM and Joshua, who had been listening in silence. She hoped they weren't worried about her having killed so many people. It wasn't like she'd had a choice.

The power of the sword was more incredible than anything she had ever experienced or expected. The way it communicated with her telling her to continue killing, made her understand why she could have turned evil. She put her hands in her pockets. "At least we no longer need to worry about Lucius." She forced a smile, unsure what to say to the two men she cared so much about.

"I am sorry that you had to be the one to destroy him," said Joshua.

Payton bit her lip. "Why do you think the sword wanted me to kill everyone around me?" she whispered, hoping no one but Joshua and Sam would hear.

"I assume the blade was created to destroy everyone except you? It seems to have more power than we realized," said Joshua.

Payton pulled her hands from her pockets and rubbed her arms at the memory. "I never want to hold it again. Nothing should have that much power."

Sam and Joshua looked troubled as they observed her.

Their enemy was defeated, and technically life could return to normal in Sylvan Falls. For Payton, the moment was not as sweet as she had hoped it would be. On the plus side, she no longer had to rely on a prophecy or destiny to make choices.

"I'm looking forward to just being an agent for the Paranormal and Supernatural Agency and not having to save the world," she laughed, hoping Sam and Joshua would lighten up a little.

When they didn't respond, she added, "I can still work here, can't I?"

Sam smiled warmly and placed his hand on her shoulder. "Of course you can. Who else is going to give me a hard time?" he teased.

"You have been through a lot in the last twelve hours. Perhaps some time away from here, resting, might be in order?" said Joshua with a small smile.

"But I'm not tired," muttered Payton.

Sam dropped his arm to his side. "Joshua is right. You have been through quite an ordeal. A couple of days off might do you some good." He smoothed the back of his head, watching her. "I wondered if you would like to stay at my place a little while longer...you know... until you feel ready to return home."

Payton hugged herself. "Gee. I hadn't thought about it, but I could use the company. To tell you the truth, I do feel out of sorts." She studied Sam's face and felt that he, too, was working through his own complicated emotions. She knew that talking things through with him might help her feel better. "I think that might be a good idea. I don't feel ready to be alone just yet. Are you sure you don't mind?" Payton asked.

Sam grinned from ear to ear. "Absolutely." His eyes shone with relief. Or was it something else? Payton was feeling too emotional to trust what she was picking up right now.

She faced her father to see a smile plastered on his face. Payton studied the handsome man with the same indigo-coloured eyes she had. "I am one lucky lady to have two amazing men like you in my life," she blurted. "Thank you for fighting alongside me today, both of you." Her eyes darted to Sam and back to her father just as Frank walked back over to them.

"How are you holding up?" Frank seemed uptight. Something Payton was unaccustomed to.

"I'm doing okay. It's a relief to know that Lucius is gone, but I'm sorry about what's happened here at Headquarters." She glanced around at the number of staff that were busily trying to create order once again.

Frank leaned in a little closer. "Azrael was right about you taking time to process what's happened. We've got things here if you want to take a couple of days off. It's been a hell of a day for you, and we have plenty of staff to help until you feel up to being here. I am pleased that we found you today."

The intensity of emotions she was picking up left her knowing without a doubt that she needed time away from the office. Payton smoothed her hair. "I am glad for the rescue and happy you still want me to work here. But I really could use a shower and a drink, to be honest... I do think I need time off."

Frank motioned to Sam with one arm. "Maybe Sam could drive you home. I'll check in with you both in a couple of days," he winked before walking away.

Payton said goodbye to her father, giving him a hug before she and Sam headed out.

BACK AT SAM'S, PAYTON showered and changed her clothes, taking some time to sit alone in her room to go over everything that had happened to this point.

Closing her eyes, her mind whirled with the events of the day. She had faced down the man that killed her family. She was beaten to a pulp. Twice. And had taken lives. Again.

These were things she would not easily or quickly forget. Payton stood and studied herself in the mirror. Outwardly, her wounds and bruises had already healed, but inside, she was a mess. Haunted by all that she had done, she prayed it would not stay with her forever. As an Immortal, forever was well and truly a very long time.

Since becoming Immortal, she had felt powerful when she needed to be. Upon holding the sword, she had become all-powerful.

Something she never wanted or asked for. The magical blade was treacherous, and she feared its effects on her could be disastrous if she was ever forced to use it again.

Letting out a ragged sigh, she went to join Sam in the living room, where he had a glass of wine waiting while he sat nursing a beer.

Payton took a seat next to him as they both stared at the floor in silence for several minutes. Finally, Payton ran her hands through her damp hair and sat back.

"Thank you again for fighting alongside me today. I didn't expect it." She moved so that she could look directly at Sam.

"I owe you....you've saved my life....How many times now?" he winked.

Payton bit her lip. "I've lost count." She giggled.

Sam smiled back at her. "Besides, it's like I've said before. We're a team. I will always have your back."

Several more minutes of silence passed between them. Payton wasn't sure if Sam wanted to talk about his feelings and was reluctant to ask. He had witnessed all that she had done, and she wondered if it changed how he felt about her now.

Unsettled and wanting to discuss her own feelings about things, Payton placed her hands on her thighs. Tilting her head, she said, "this morning, I had a stalker and a destiny to fulfil. Now everything is different. I'm not sure what is expected of me or what I am supposed to do next?"

Sam looked surprised by her statement. "Nothing is *expected* of you by anyone. Your life is your own now, Payton. You can do whatever you want." Sam's voice was gentle.

"I killed people today. I never wanted to do that again." Payton's voice cracked.

Sam reached out and took her hand in his, giving it a gentle squeeze. "You did what you had to do. It doesn't make you evil. None of what happened is your fault. You didn't ask for any of it."

Payton lowered her head. Her eyes were hooded when she made eye contact with him again. "Do you feel differently about me now that you saw what I am capable of?" she whispered, fearing the answer he would give.

Sam leaned closer, lifting her chin with his finger, urging her to make eye contact. She chewed her bottom lip as he spoke. "I saw the thrashing Lucius gave you before you used the sword, as well as the bruises from his earlier beating. It tore my heart out to see you hurt. Believe me, if I could have killed him myself, I would have," he admitted.

Payton sniffed. She fought back the urge to blubber. It would seem she had not destroyed things with Sam after all.

Sam looked away for a moment as if in thought. When he brought his gaze back to hers, he said, "Joshua told me he thought I could somehow help you remain on the side of light. But from what I saw today, your fortitude is incredible. You don't need me to keep you from going all dark side."

Payton closed her eyes. It was only at that moment that she realized the truth. Joshua was right. Sam was her anchor to remain in the light. Lucius had somehow known it, or he wouldn't have tried to have Sam killed.

She could hear Sam sigh. "I don't know if you even realize how strong you are, Miss Adams."

Payton opened her eyes to see a wide grin on Sam's face. His eyes sparkled. She couldn't help but smile back.

"It's time you realize how incredible you are. You've said it yourself. You are one of a kind." Sam winked.

Payton realized he was still holding her hand, and she was reluctant to pull it away.

"That's not what I meant... I meant I am the only Immortal Witch...."

"I know what you meant," he whispered. "You are still incredible."

"You are pretty amazing yourself, Samuel Clements," she said, giving his hand a squeeze before sitting back.

CHAPTER TWENTY-FIVE

FOUR MONTHS LATER.

Things had returned to normal in The Agency and in Sylvan Falls. Shops were now reopened, and the town was buzzing with excitement and joy once again. After staying with Sam for a week after the incident downtown, Payton returned to her own home.

Payton's friendship with Sam was going great. She really wanted a different kind of relationship with him now, though. Especially since things in her life looked as though they would finally be normal. Well, normal for her. Her feelings for him continued to grow, and she found it hard to keep them to herself.

She was happy when her father moved in with her since there was no longer a need to keep his presence secret from the townspeople. Azrael remained in town, continuing to live in the extra rooms in Sylvan Falls Museum. She occasionally trained with him but found that sparring with Sam was much more fun.

In fact, any chance she had to be around Sam was blissful.

There was one snag, however. Wherever Payton went, people gawked at her with curiosity and wonder. It was becoming slightly more bearable than the first few weeks.

It appeared everyone looked up to her, thinking she was some kind of superhero. She hoped that over time, the interest in her would die down.

It turned out that about a hundred items of various sizes and power were missing from the vault. Payton had personally logged every artifact in the storage facility and took it as a personal affront that the items were now missing.

She and Frank knew the artifacts would need to be retrieved, but they did not know where to begin their search.

Some of the objects were cursed, while others were imbibed with powerful magic. Dangerous in the wrong hands, to be sure. She just hoped every single missing item would be found without incident but knew that was wishful thinking.

LEAVING THE GYM WITH Sam, Payton asked, "How do you feel about coming over tonight for dinner? Dad says he's going to cook." She tucked hair behind her ears.

"As long as *you* aren't cooking," Sam teased.

"You're one to talk." Payton playfully punched his arm while Sam laughed. They both stopped in their tracks when they saw Frank approaching them.

"Payton. Sam. I would like you to meet our two newest recruits," said Frank.

Standing on either side of Frank was a man and a woman. Both appeared to be in their mid-twenties.

"This is Erwin and Angela. They are our first warlock and witch Agents, aside from you. I was hoping you could mentor them?"

Payton looked first at Erwin. He was handsome with a cleft in his chin and a roman nose. He had shoulder-length chocolate brown hair and stood a few inches shorter than Payton. "What type of warlock are you?" she asked.

Erwin stood at attention. "Earth magic, ma'am."

Payton stifled a laugh. Sam laughed out loud, and she slapped his bicep. "Call me Payton. And what about you, Angela?"

Angela looked star-struck. Payton groaned inwardly. The curvy young woman had large eyes and bright auburn-coloured hair, tinted with gold. "I'm a water witch," Lucy bubbled.

Payton looked at Frank. "What is it you want me to mentor them in exactly?" she asked, knowing that Agent training was very well rounded in most areas. Except for magic.

"I'd like them to help you locate the lost vault artifacts. Answer questions they may have... that sort of thing." Frank nodded.

She could feel Sam watching her. "That sounds fine. Let's go to the cafeteria and catch up before we get to work," said Payton, hearing Sam's stomach rumble.

The trio headed into the cafeteria as Payton's phone rang. Seeing that it was Di, Payton answered. "Hi, Di. What's up?"

"I think I have something here that may interest you?" Di said in a low voice.

"Oh? What's that?" asked Payton.

"Someone came in offering to sell me what looks like an innocent-looking stone goddess statue. As soon as I held it, I knew it was much more. You need to come down here," Di disclosed.

"Is the seller still there?" asked Payton.

"No. I bought the item because I think it is too dangerous to be in the hands of just anyone."

Payton was intrigued. "I'll be there shortly." She hung up and looked at Sam, who had just ordered some food.

She pointed upward. "Di may have one of our artifacts. I won't be gone long."

Sam tilted his head with an amused expression on his face. "Fine, but if you will not wait for me, maybe you should take these two with you?"

Payton chuckled when she glanced at Erwin and Angela's eager faces. "Okay. Let's go, you two." She smiled at Sam. "Enjoy your food. I won't be gone long."

He winked and grabbed his plate.

THE TRIO REACHED DI'S shop in no time, and they followed Payton into the magic and coffee shop.

After a few introductions, Di ushered them to the back of the store. She went into the back storage area and returned seconds later, holding a white goddess statue.

Payton could see the change in Di's aura when she approached, holding the item.

"Here." Di handed the item over to Payton, who took it into her hands. She immediately felt the buzzing energy emitting from the statue. It was evident that it had been imbibed with powerful magic, but there was more to it than that. She looked at Di with one eyebrow cocked.

"Cursed?" she asked her friend.

"I think so." Di put her hands on her hips.

Payton closed her eyes and focused on the object. Images flashed in her mind, as well as feeling the creator of the statue. Opening her eyes, she stared into Di's.

"Did you see a campfire and hear the incantations?" Payton asked.

Di nodded.

"I don't understand Latin. What is the person saying?"

Di took the statue in her hands again, then spoke. "The translation is, with fire and earth, protect me from my enemies. But then she asks for control over her future."

"That doesn't sound so bad?" said Payton.

"The problem is there is one more part... Qui impugnat perdere me... It means to destroy all who oppose me."

Payton was surprised. She had felt animosity from the object, but it didn't feel evil... exactly. Its effect on Di's aura made sense now.

Di added. "This statue, if used by the wrong person, could destroy anyone they feel opposes them." She shook her head.

Payton pulled out a bag from her pocket and placed the statue inside of it.

Angela spoke up. "Isn't there a way to negate the spell or neutralize it?" she asked.

Di shook her head. "This feels like it was created at least a hundred years ago. There is no way of knowing who the creator was. Typically, it is difficult to negate the magic spells of others. Especially one who practices the dark arts."

"Could we cast another spell upon it that would be stronger than the original one?" asked Erwin.

Payton smiled. "All good questions, but the truth is that The Agency prefers to keep these kinds of magical items out of the public domain. It is safer for everyone that way."

Her new colleagues nodded but remained silent.

"What did the seller look like? Have you seen them before?" Payton asked Di.

"A man about five-foot-six, dark hair. He wasn't a warlock. I think he may have been some type of supernatural."

"Would you know him if you saw him?"

Di nodded. "I believe I would, yes."

Payton called Bryce in operations. "Hi. Can you send me the file of suspects that escaped custody after the vault break-in?"

Several minutes later, Payton's phone pinged. She opened the file with the images of a half-dozen men and women suspected of stealing from the vault. Handing her phone to Di, she watched her friend scroll through the pictures.

"That's him." Di pointed. Taking back her phone, Payton thanked Di, and the trio headed outside.

"What now?" asked Angela.

"Now we take this back to HQ and put it in the vault. Then we check with Ops to see if facial recognition has located the thief."

SAM LOOKED UP FROM his desk and smiled when Payton entered their office. The other Agents were out, and it was just her and Sam for the moment. She took a seat at her desk and filled him in on the first artifact retrieval since the many items were stolen.

"I am sure all the items will turn up at some point." Sam smiled.

"Let's just hope that shopkeepers like Di let us know if they come across anything weird. I've already sent a memo to the pawnshop in town, but so far, they have reported nothing strange."

Sam turned in his chair, and Payton did the same so they could talk face to face.

Payton smacked her forehead with her palm when she remembered something. "There is one thing I forgot to mention earlier... When dad and I were on our way to work this morning, Azrael texted me. He wants to see me this afternoon for a meeting."

"Any idea what it's about?" Sam's brows raised.

"No, but Joshua is insisting on joining us, so I am not convinced it's good news. I hope it isn't another prophecy." Payton shuddered at the thought.

"What do you mean? What could it be? You fulfilled your destiny. What more can be asked of you?" Sam's brow creased.

"That's what scares me, Sam. I honestly don't know why he would want a meeting with me. It sounds very official." She put her head down and closed her eyes. Payton had barely begun to deal with the feelings around the events downtown four months earlier and the lives she had taken.

She looked back over at Sam and frowned. "My life is finally feeling normal. I'm happy. All I want to do is my job as an Agent and work cases with you."

Sam stood and walked to her, placing a hand on her shoulder. "I'm coming with you to the meeting. Whatever it's about, you will not go through it alone."

Payton looked up at Sam. "I don't expect you to go with me...." She chewed the inside of her cheek, grateful for the offer.

Sam smoothed Payton's hair. His eyes were tender. "Nonsense. I won't take no for an answer."

Payton stood. "I don't know what I would do without you, Sam. After everything we've been through... The fact that you still want to be there for me... Thank you." She bit her lip.

Sam put his hand on his heart. "I know you are capable and independent. You don't need my help, and technically, you have been the one saving *my* ass all the time. But I will always be here for you, no matter what. You have come to mean a lot to me. I wouldn't-"

Payton cut him off, throwing herself into his arms. Sam responded by wrapping his arms around her, holding her tight. Their bodies were closer than they had ever been during a hug.

Being near him this way filled Payton with hope for her future. She held on, inhaling his scent, trying to calm her pounding heart. The faint smell of aftershave, the outdoors, and his own gorgeous scent had the opposite effect of calm.

In an instant, Sam's energy changed from a supportive partner to something else. She'd felt it before from him, and each time she had pretended not to. *Not this time.* She loved this man, and she couldn't deny it any longer. Sam needed to know how she felt about him.

Payton pulled her head back just enough that she could feel his breath on her face. Sam's eyes flashed with intensity as they searched hers, seeking permission to kiss her.

Payton's mouth went dry, and she licked her lips as their eyes remained locked.

Sam's hand moved to the back of her head, his fingers threaded through her hair. He leaned in and pressed his lips softly against hers. The kiss deepened, and a low moan escaped them both.

When the kiss was over, Payton felt a warmth rising inside her. She smoothed her fingertips along her bottom lip. "I can't believe..." she murmured.

Sam cleared his throat. His mouth curved into a smile. "What can't you believe? That I feel the same way you do?"

Payton gave a silent nod, her eyes wide. "I was about to tell you I'm crazy about you," she giggled.

"I fell for you from the moment I first saw you," Sam admitted, moving his brows up and down.

Payton looked at him in surprise. "I thought I just annoyed you with my stubbornness?" she smirked and giggled again.

Sam reached out and smoothed her hair. "You did. But I love how you are so strong. I wouldn't change anything about you."

Payton beamed from ear to ear. "I... I've known no one that makes me feel so happy," she confessed.

Their eyes locked again, and Payton wanted nothing more than to continue kissing him but also didn't want one of the other Agents to walk in on them.

She smiled at Sam, unsure of what else to say. They had finally kissed, and it was a toe-curling kiss at that.

She took a couple of steps back, then looked at the clock on the wall. "The meeting... It's time... We should go," Payton said, pointing to the door with a permanent grin on her face.

Sam grinned back, following her out of the office.

PAYTON AND SAM ARRIVED at the meeting room at the same time as Joshua. They all entered the room and took a seat.

"Good afternoon, Azrael." Payton smiled when she saw him seated at the round table. Fear fluttered in her stomach when she saw he looked troubled. Azrael nodded a hello, observing Joshua and Sam for a brief moment. Sam and her father took a seat on either side of her.

She sensed her father did not fully trust Azrael, as he may once have. Payton wasn't sure what Azrael's agenda was or if he still had one, but she didn't feel he intended harm to come to her. At least she hoped not. Payton liked him and still considered him her mentor. He may have withheld information from her, but looking back, she could understand why he did it.

She held her breath. Azrael's usual stoic expression was replaced with one of unease. "Something worrisome has come to my attention. Word of Payton single-handedly stopping Lucius and the other Fallen Immortals has caused quite a stir. The shifter council here in Sylvan Falls sent word to the European Shifter Commission. It would seem that they, in turn, notified an Immortal who is part of the Governing body of Immortal Guardians."

Payton asked, "who is this governing body? This is the first I've been told of them."

Azrael continued, "they are a collective of original Immortal Guardians who oversee our work on this planet. They ensure we are following the guidelines laid out from our home worlds overseers."

Joshua shoved his shoulders back, placing his palms down on the table. "Do they know she is my daughter?"

Azrael's lips were a thin line, "they know she is Immortal and a witch."

"What difference does it make whose daughter I am?" asked Payton, not liking where this was going.

"None. It only matters that you are an Immortal with powerful magic. In other words, the one mentioned in the old prophecy," Azrael stated.

Joshua shook his head. "Do they also know about the sword?"

Azrael looked pensive. "Only myself and a handful of Immortal Guardians ever knew of it. None were aware of where it was hidden." He gestured toward Payton, "until a few months ago when I retrieved it for Payton. Now that Payton has used it, I am sure they will be interested in getting their hands on it."

Sam interrupted, putting a palm up. "What happens if they come for the sword? I thought no one could wield it, but Payton?"

"They will not find the sword. However, we have a bigger problem," Azrael pursed his lips. "There is something I failed to mention before because it did not seem relevant to do so." He swallowed hard before continuing, which only irritated Payton.

"It is about the prophecy. I feel it is important that you know *all* the details around its creation and its creator." Azrael clasped his hands on top of the table.

Bile rose in Payton's throat at the mention of the word prophecy. Her dreams about the blacksmith and Lucius had stopped months ago. *Now what?* "Don't tell me there is more that I must do?" she gulped.

Her eyes darted to Sam, who sat next to her. He was frowning and looking as annoyed as she felt. Another revelation about her was not what she wanted to hear. Looking back at Azrael for an explanation, she bit her lip.

"There is nothing you must do. However, you should know that the blacksmith who created the sword and cursed it was your ancestor. He was a Chartwell."

Payton gasped. "What? You didn't think it was relevant to tell me I was related to the creator of the sword of power?"

Joshua hung his head and let out a frustrated sigh. Payton wondered if he had also known. Sam was silent while Payton just shook her head, waiting for more bad news she sensed was coming.

Azrael sat up straight and looked Payton in the eye as he spoke. "Lucius had many dealings with the Chartwells over the centuries. As a result, the Immortal Guardians do not trust the Chartwell name. They feel all Chartwells are easily manipulated by the Fallen Immortals."

Joshua slammed a palm down on the table. "She wasn't manipulated. Lucius failed in his plans to turn her," he insisted.

Azrael put both hands up, his face stern. "I agree with you, brother. Payton chose her side. But now that they have been made aware of her, we must prepare ourselves. They will be coming for her and the sword."

"I don't understand? What do you mean they are coming for her? Why?" asked Sam with wide eyes.

A chill ran through Payton when she remembered what Lucius had told her. He said the Immortal Guardians would fear her and either imprison her or use her as a weapon. It would seem he had not lied about that.

She wondered if Azrael had worried about this all along? Is that why he chose not to speak of it with her?

Payton felt her anger grow for the first time since the killing of Lucius. "I will not use the sword, and I will not be taken prisoner by anyone!" she slammed her fist onto the table.

Sam spoke up, his voice strained, "do they not realize she is more powerful than any of them? Surely they don't think they can take her or the sword?"

Payton stroked the nape of her neck, her bottom lip quivering. "I thought this was over. Can't you speak to the Guardians and explain to them I am no threat?" Her eyes moistened with tears as she looked at Azrael.

Azrael shook his head. "Regrettably, I fear it will be not only Immortal Guardians but also Fallen Immortals who will seek you out. Lucius has friends who aren't happy that he is gone." Azrael closed his eyes for a moment. His expression darkened.

"What does this mean for Payton? What can we do?" asked Sam.

Payton's heart sank, and she put her hands to her face, unprepared for the news that Immortals were coming for her.

Sam put an arm around her. "I won't let anything happen to you."

Azrael stood tall. "Anyone that comes looking for you will have to face *us*."

He nodded at Joshua, who was already standing. Their faces were fierce with determination. Payton felt a sense of pride and courage in knowing that they would fight alongside her. It was easy to forget that these Immortal Guardians were also warriors. She was glad to have them on her side.

"Let them come," Joshua threatened.

The End

Thank you for reading Immortal Choices. I hope you enjoyed it.

I would be grateful if you left a review on the platform[1] you purchased the book from. As an Indie author, reviews help me get my books in front of the people who will enjoy them.

Thank you,

Tori

Want to be the first to hear about special offers, giveaways and free content? Sign up for my newsletter.[2]

I will also announce future upcoming books on my website[3].

If you prefer to only be notified when I release a new book, you can follow me on BookBub[4]. You may also follow me on Facebook[5] and Instagram[6].

---

1. https://books2read.com/u/3JZnaP
2. https://www.torirayne.com/newsletter/
3. https://www.torirayne.com/
4. https://www.bookbub.com/authors/tori-rayne
5. https://www.facebook.com/toriraynefantasywriter
6. https://www.instagram.com/authortorirayne/

About the Author

Tori has been writing stories for decades and has always been an avid reader of mysteries, the paranormal, thrillers, fantasy, science fiction and historical romance.

She enjoys writing fiction books that combine Magic, Fantasy, Metaphysical and the Paranormal. She has recently written a new Urban Fantasy Series.

You may reach Tori at tori@torirayne.com

Read more at www.torirayne.com.

CPSIA information can be obtained
at www.ICGtesting.com
Printed in the USA
LVHW011003181221
706489LV00017B/1258

9 780995 247192